Praise for Heidi Cullinan & Marie Sexton's
Family Man

"...they capture the beauty of developing a relationship based on mutual interest without resorting to immediate gratuitous sex (although the eventual sex is steamy) in an homage to the old-fashioned romance."

~ *Library Journal*

"Warm and romantic and touching and sexy. I loved both Trey and Vince and they are both just so *good* that I couldn't help but want the best for them. Excellent story and one that I highly recommend."

~ *Joyfully Jay*

"*Family Man* has so many things going for it I couldn't help but love it. [...] The partnership of Marie Sexton and Heidi Cullinan brought all the best things about their work together into one delightful book. I can't recommend *Family Man* highly enough."

~ *Joyfully Reviewed*

Look for these titles by
Heidi Cullinan

Now Available:

A Private Gentleman
Love Lessons

Minnesota Christmas
Let It Snow

Special Delivery
Special Delivery
Double Blind

Family Man

Heidi Cullinan & Marie Sexton

SAMHAIN
PUBLISHING

Samhain Publishing, Ltd.
11821 Mason Montgomery Road, 4B
Cincinnati, OH 45249
www.samhainpublishing.com

Family Man
Copyright © 2014 by Heidi Cullinan & Marie Sexton
Print ISBN: 978-1-61921-690-7
Digital ISBN: 978-1-61921-466-8

Editing by Sasha Knight
Cover by Angela Waters

First Samhain Publishing, Ltd. electronic publication: March 2013
First Samhain Publishing, Ltd. print publication: March 2014

Acknowledgment

Thanks to Dan, Lisa and Jo for being outstanding beta readers as always.

Dedication

For everyone who's stuck on the merry-go-round. We wish we could give you all big fat Italian families.

Chapter One

I don't care how poor a man is. If he has family, he's rich.
— *Dan Wilcox and Thad Mumford*

The truth about Vincent Fierro's sexual orientation came to him as he lay underneath a client's sink, de-clogging onion skins from a busted garbage disposal in a two-bedroom condo on Aldine. *I wonder,* he mused, *if maybe I'm gay.*

The thought made him jerk his head back against the sink trap hard enough to give him a goose egg, and he swore under his breath as he tried to push the alarming idea away and focus on the job at hand. Though the job was tedious, it was uncomplicated, and no sooner had he dismissed the dark little thought it was back again.

It was stupid. Vince knew he wasn't gay.

He blamed the onion fumes and his rumbling stomach, imagining them tangling with the knowledge he hadn't had a date in a month and hadn't been laid since Cara Paglia had taken him home to cheer him up after his last divorce, which had been in October. It had been too long since he'd given the old boy a ride, so long that answering a call for a gay married couple made him think for one idiot second that maybe that was his problem, why he had broken his mama's heart with divorce number three. That maybe his problem was that he was looking in the wrong pasture.

Vince rolled his eyes at himself and pulled out more onion goop. It was middle age, that's what it was. It was his sister-in-law the beautician suggesting at dinner the night before that he let her start coloring and highlighting his hair now while the gray was just barely noticeable. It was realizing a couple days a week at the gym and walking from Emilio's to his brother's house every other Sunday wasn't enough to keep his three-year-old niece from asking if she could rest her head on his "nice squishy tummy" while they watched *Tangled* for the fiftieth time. It was finding out kids born the year he graduated high school were now legal to drink. It was his latest ex-wife leaving him for a twenty-eight-year-old.

It was *not* because he was gay. Because Vince wasn't gay. You didn't marry three women and sleep with how many others and then decide—with your head under a sink and your eyes stinging of onion—that since you were thirty-eight and single you must be gay. Sex with another man wasn't just some random idea to try on when you'd gone through everything else.

Of course the little devil in the back of his mind had to whisper, *It isn't exactly a random idea, now, is it, Vinnie?*

Clearing his throat and mentally drop-kicking the devil back to the rock he lived under, Vince pulled the last of the onion muck out of the housing, wiped his hands on a towel and aimed his flashlight at the naked unit. His brain was blissfully occupied now with assessing rings and seals, and he grimaced as he saw both the blade and the hopper would need to be replaced. Given the unit itself was almost old enough to drink, they'd be better off getting a new one. Pushing himself out from inside the cupboard, Vince adjusted his T-shirt and followed the sound of voices down the hall to give his clients the news. He stopped outside the closed door to the home office, however, caught up in the hushed tones of their conversation.

"—feel so stupid. Why do onion skins clog a sink? Isn't that what a garbage disposal is *for?*"

"It doesn't matter. Maybe it's just old. Maybe the new ones can take it no problem. Don't beat yourself up, sweetheart."

"We don't have the money for this, Kyle. Not with me laid off. God, but I wish—" The speaker broke off, and Vince thought he caught a muffled sigh.

"Shh. Hush. It's going to be all right. You're going to get another job. And if we don't replace the disposal right away, then we'll just do without for a little while."

"That's all we're doing, living without. And it's all my fault—"

The first man was quite clearly near tears, but Kyle only got calmer and gentler the more upset his partner became. "It is *not* your fault. It's the slimy sub-prime mortgagers and those assholes who made trading their shit a game who started this."

"I should never have switched jobs. Never. If I'd stayed at First Union, I'd have seniority, and I'd still have a job."

"Bill, *stop*. You're making yourself crazy over a clogged sink."

"That's what I feel like! A clogged man." Vince heard the speaker choke back a sob before adding in an angry whisper, "I don't know what the fuck you still see in me. I wouldn't even blame you if you went off with some hot young thing with healthy self-esteem, a full head of hair and a job."

"If he had good health-insurance benefits and a low-mileage vehicle, I might be tempted." On the other side of the door, Vince imagined Kyle lifting the other man's chin and staring him in the face as he spoke. "Honey, I know this is rough. And I know damn well I'd be the same kind of wreck if it'd been me laid off for eighteen months. But you have to stop beating yourself up. You didn't break the garbage disposal. It just broke. You didn't make a bad move on your job. You just got screwed. And I don't care if you lose every hair on your head and gain twenty pounds. I love you, I married you, and you're going to have to work a lot harder than this to get rid of me."

No more sounds came from the room into the hallway except the occasional soft *smack* of lips parting and reuniting at a new angle. Vincent slipped quietly back to the kitchen, where he leaned on the wall next to the fridge and shut his eyes against the strange ache inside him.

That. He wanted *that.* Even as he reassured himself *that* was just a healthy relationship he'd heard, not a magical gay relationship, he couldn't stop the deeper, more aching whisper from rising up inside him. *I want a man to treat me like that.*

Pushing the thought away in a panic, he headed back down the hallway, louder this time, clearing his throat and rapping smartly on the wood. The taller blond man opened it, moving to shield his partner from view as he blew his nose noisily into a tissue. "Finished already?"

Vince cleared his throat a second time. "Here's the deal. It's an old unit. I'm not gonna lie. A good chunk of the guts are dull or near to useless. The clog didn't help much, but all it did was point out trouble that was already there."

The man grimaced. "I see. So we need a new unit."

"Well, that's the thing." Vince rubbed the back of his neck. "It'd be best, yeah. But if you wanted, you could limp this along a bit longer, if you were careful. I can jimmy the blade a bit, buy you time. It'd mean you'd be putting a lot of junk you'd normally send down the disposal into the trash instead until you replaced it. No onion skins. No potato peels or carrot shreds. But soggy cereal, pasta—anything that isn't stringy or sticky or hard—would be okay in small batches and with a lot of water. Give it extra time to chop, 'cause it'll need it. And in the meantime, you can save up for what you want. Do some research on how powerful you want it and then watch for a sale. I'll leave some names for brands to watch for and ones to avoid. When you get what you want, give us a call and we'll install it."

The blond man didn't answer right away, meeting Vince's gaze instead as he took it all in. A silent conversation seemed to follow.

Heard us, did you?

Yep. Just trying to help. Know what it's like.

And you don't mind that we're gay, big burly Italian boy like you?

Vince shrugged and averted his eyes.

"Thank you," the man said. "I believe we'll take your advice and limp along until we can save up. That was very thoughtful of you to suggest such a plan."

"Not a problem." Vince jerked his head toward the kitchen. "I'll clean up and do a quick job on the blade. You want to put a cake pan or something under it for tonight. It shouldn't leak, but if it does, that means you start shopping right now."

"I will," the man promised.

Vince felt good about himself for helping people in a tight spot, trying not to think of all the crazy shit he kept trying to think of instead. He was doing really well all the way up until he was scribbling brand names on the back of a business card and the blond man came into the kitchen holding out an envelope. "I want you to have these. They're vouchers for tickets to a theater I manage down on Broadway."

Vince held up a hand in protest. "You don't have to do that."

"I do." The man smiled. "I can't tell you how grateful I am. I know you heard us talking about money. And I also know you haven't so much as batted an eye at the fact that we're gay men."

"Well, we are in Lakeview," Vince said, voice heavy with meaning, and hoped he didn't have to finish the rest of that sentence.

"You'd be surprised." He thrust the tickets at Vince again. "Please. They're good anytime from now until the rest of the year. Consider them a token of my sincere appreciation. And stop by the office if you use them. I'll make sure you get good seats and complimentary drinks for the night."

Not knowing what else to do, Vince took the envelope with a gruff nod.

The man caught his hand and squeezed it gently. "I hope

someday someone gives you the kind of lift you gave me and my husband tonight. And be sure of it, I'll be using Parino Brothers Plumbing from now on."

Vince escaped shortly after that, leaving his card and a bill and accepting a check and two enthusiastic handshakes before heading back to the van. The strange flush of emotions and potential self-discoveries went back to the shop with him, and they followed him home as well, lingering through his solitary meal, a soak in the tub and all the way through two glasses of brandy.

Chapter Two

The nagging questions about Vince's sexuality lingered even a few days later, and he blamed them for his desire to stop by his family's restaurant without so much as a guilt trip from his mother.

Emilio's Cafe had been on the corner of Taylor and Morgan since 1952 when Vince's grandfather had kept his promise to give his wife a "little place to show off the best Italian cooking in Chicago" as soon as he got back from the war. He'd been back from the war for several years by then, obviously, but Giorgio Fierro had forgotten to check the price of Little Italy real estate before he'd made his bold vow. Which was why the cafe hadn't been named Marisa's Cafe as he'd planned but Emilio's, after his great uncle who he'd finally persuaded to lend him the money on the condition of free meals for life and his name emblazoned on the sign above the roll-out awning. And the placemats, and the napkins, and the matchboxes and even on the glasses and coffee cups, the latter two which were still stolen by college students wanting to take home a souvenir of their favorite hangout.

Plenty of University of Illinois students littered the restaurant when Vince stopped by, most taking up the big curving booths in the back, but a group sat at the big circular table in the middle and several dotted the bar as well. Uncle Frank was manning that station, his wild salt-and-pepper (though mostly salt at this point) hair sticking out in at least seven directions, further solidifying his legend as "the crazy old man who puts hot sauce in your drink if he thinks you gave him a fake ID." If only the kids knew how later Frank would go home and get teary over Lifetime Movies of the Week.

When Frank saw Vince come in, he stopped glowering at his customers long enough to give his nephew a nod.

"Vinnie!" The cry was the only warning Vince got before his cousin Vera tackled him from behind in a hug. Then she *whapped* him on the arm with a dishtowel. "What do you think you're doing, not coming by the cafe for so long?" She'd moved in front of him now, her dark eyes narrowing beneath her wild mane of soft-permed hair. "You been eating at that Greek place again? Is that it?"

"He comes in," Frank said as he wiped out a glass. "Just not when you're working."

Vera hit Vince with her dishtowel again.

Vince held up his hands and backed away. "Easy, easy! I been on a job up in Skokie. A complete refit of six condos. Had a call in Lakeview Tuesday too. I barely get anywhere these days." Vera mellowed somewhat, and he pressed his advantage. "How are the kids doing? Does Davy have a game coming up I could go see?"

"Saturday." Vera beamed. "You should have seen him last week. Hit a home run and a triple in the same inning. And in the last he nailed a line drive so hard it knocked the shortstop on his ass."

"Well, tell him Cousin Vinnie expects to see somebody go to the hospital on Saturday."

Vera laughed and bussed a kiss on his cheek. "It's good to see you, Vin. Don't you be a stranger no more."

He barely sat down at a table before the door to the kitchen burst open and more family came out. This one was his niece and goddaughter, Marcie, wearing her waitress uniform and a shy, pretty smile that hid her braces. "Hi, Uncle Vinnie." As she passed a group of college kids, a straw wrapper hit her in the side of the face, and she staggered back, blushing as red as the placemats.

Every male member of the Fierro family acted at once. Frank was bellowing from behind the bar and shuffling arthritically to the pass-through as Marcie's older brother set his busboy tub on a table and started weaving through chairs, but Vince, only two tables over, beat them all and moved to loom over the well-groomed and tanned blond idiot.

"You got some sort of problem?" Vince asked, his voice making it very clear, that yes, the blond idiot did.

Predictably, the idiot went for machismo. "It was just a stupid gag. Jesus."

An angry gasp from behind Vince told him that his Uncle Marco had come out from the kitchen in time to hear the blasphemy.

Vince leaned over the empty chair at the great circular table and glared at the blond idiot. "Apologize."

The idiot blinked. "What?"

"Apologize," Marco said, angry where Vince had been quietly threatening. "To Marcie and to the Son of God, you lousy son of a bitch!"

"Marco, Vincent—what on Earth are you doing?"

It was Lisa, Vince's mom. She came out of the kitchen and stared at them all with her hands on her hips. "Well? Answer me!"

"This punk was picking on Marcie," Marco said.

"I was not! It was an accident!"

Lisa reached out and smacked each one of them on the side of the head, one after the other. Vince, then Frank, then Marco. "What are you, a bunch of Fierro hooligans again, running around the neighborhood, beating up anybody who looks at your sisters twice?"

"But, Ma—" Vince started to say.

"Enough. Go sit down."

Fierro men may have been tough, but nobody was going to question Lisa. The men all hung their head like boys and backed up a step. The blond punk started to laugh.

Smack.

Vince was pretty sure his mom had smacked the kid far harder than she'd smacked him.

"What the hell?" the kid yelled.

"You don't get off the hook so easy. Just because I kept them from beating you to a pulp doesn't mean you don't owe my granddaughter an apology."

The blond blushed. "Sorry."

Lisa's hand slapped him squarely in the back of the head this time, almost pitching him into his lemonade. "Stand up, boy, and say it like you mean it."

The boy did, scooting his chair back, his face now much redder than Marcie's. "I'm very sorry, miss. I was rude, and it won't happen again." A grunt from Marco had him adding quickly, "And I'm sorry, Jesus, for taking your name in vain."

"Good boy," Lisa said, patting him on the head. "Enjoy your meal."

She turned and left. Marco and Frank nodded. Marcie hurried back to the kitchen. She was mortified, Vince knew.

Tough. Nobody messed with Fierro girls. Nobody.

The Fierros dispersed, all of them casting independent warning glances as they returned to their previous positions. On his way back to the table, Vince grabbed a newspaper and hid behind it as he sat down, pretending to read while he listened intently to the heated whispers. He caught "Holy shit!" and "What the fuck was that?" and "Jesus, I'm never coming *here* again," and then a familiar voice, much louder said, "What the hell did you guys do while I was in the bathroom?"

Vince lowered his paper enough to peer over the top of it. Yep. It was Trey Giles slipping into the empty chair Vince had been leaning over.

The chair beside him scraped back, and Frank sat down in it. "What's a nice boy like little Trey doing with that pack of *baboos?*" He glowered at the table. "I should go call his grandma right now."

"Hush." Vince settled firmly behind the paper again. "I'm trying to listen."

Someone was just wrapping up a retelling of the scene. "God, Trey, I thought you said this was a *good* place."

"It is. And I hope you haven't screwed it up, because I want to come back here again."

Frank clucked his tongue. "Like we'd ever keep Sophia's grandson away."

"*Hush,*" Vince hissed.

"But you did apologize, right?" Trey was asking. "And they seemed satisfied?"

"I guess." That was the blond idiot.

"Listen, man. You're going to leave a huge tip. I mean *huge.* I won't have the Fierros thinking I'm hanging with schmucks who are rude *and* cheap." The idiot gurgled a protest, but Trey ran over him. "You'll do that, or you'll be finishing this project on your own. Got it? Because you all know I'm the one carrying us on this anyway." The rest Vince couldn't catch, as Trey was murmuring it under his breath, but it was clear he was pissed.

Vince smiled and lowered the paper.

Frank nodded, looking satisfied. "Such a nice young man. So good to his granny." He pulled a handkerchief from his shirt pocket and dabbed at his eye. Then he frowned at the empty place in front of Vince. "Marcie didn't take your order." He rose, slowly, his creaky joints making the task a chore. "You want a scotch? Yes. Yes. I'll get you a scotch."

"Thanks, Uncle Frank," Vince said, wishing he could give the older man a hand. He wasn't even old. Not old enough to hurt like he did. But he'd been rheumy since Vince had been the one getting dressed down for being a *baboo* in the cafe, and now Frank practically had a ninety-year-old body instead of the sixty-five-year-old he should.

But he had enough pride for ten Italian men, so Vince said nothing, just let Frank get him a double. In the time that had taken, Marcie had come back out and asked if Vince wanted the special or his usual. After glancing at the board and seeing the special was spinach ravioli, he ordered the special. Marcie went back to the kitchen, and Vince read a few sections of the paper before Frank came back with his scotch. He sat down once again, settling in for a chat.

"Vera's right," he said, leaning back with a shot of his own. "You don't come by often enough. And I know you ain't eating at the downtown place, because they think you're coming here."

Vince suppressed the urge to sigh. "Neither of you are in my neighborhood, and I work in Northbrook."

Frank made a face. "You work for a fool. Why don't you come work with your family?"

"Jack's my uncle too."

"Bah." Frank waved the idea away with his hand. "The Parinos. They don't know what family is. They all live in the suburbs, and none of them the same one. You should live here, Vinnie. Here with your family." He gestured to the round table. "Like little Trey Oscar, taking care of Sophia and his mother."

Vince said nothing, only took a sip of his scotch.

Frank kept talking. "Four generations. Four generations work here, Vinnie. How many families can say that, eh? How many families stay that close? You should come back. There's a condo opening up down the street from *your* grandmother, bless her heart. Live there and work here."

"I have a job," Vince pointed out.

"A job that works you too hard. And I know you're thinking of leaving. You're always thinking of leaving. You should. Come back to the restaurant. You could take over the books from your cousin Lou. God bless him, but he can't add worth a damn."

Vince didn't do the books anymore, because he knew damn well what should have been simple accounting also came with being the organizer-in-chief and being everyone's errand boy. He also knew from long experience that this conversation wouldn't get any better, so he changed the subject. "How's Amanda and the new baby?"

Frank's eyes lit up. "Ah. He's a feisty one. Never wants to nap. Drives his mama crazy." He launched into stories about his daughter and her third baby, the first boy, and Vince listened, generally interested.

As Marcie came out with his order and Frank's stories drifted into the more mundane retellings of what neighbors had come to the cafe for breakfast, his mind began to drift back, as it had so often this week, to the Lakeview job, to the couple again. The same feelings of confusion and longing filled him, and he realized that instead of curing them, being in the den of his family only made them worse. He felt lonely. He felt cut off.

He felt wrong. Like everything he was doing was wrong.

His eyes slid over to the round table, where even the blond idiot was carrying on about how good Marco's cooking was. He saw the boys leaning on the girls and the girls flirting with the boys. He saw them all laughing and talking, all connected. All happy.

Well, they were all hooked up except for Trey, but then Trey was never hooked up with anyone. If he did hook up, Vince doubted it would be with one of these girls, who were all clearly rich kids from the suburbs. No, it'd be with that girl from that group he always came in with.

Though as Vince thought about it, there were more guys than girls in that group, and the guys were always hanging all over each other. He'd figured it was just being friendly.

What if it wasn't? What if Trey were...?

Well, what if? What the hell would it matter to you?

Vince didn't know. He felt embarrassed, then felt foolish for being embarrassed. He needed to get out more. He needed to get *laid.*

Gaze drifting back to Trey, Vince took in Trey's shining blond hair, which fell into his eyes as he reached over a book in his lap to take a bite of ravioli.

Vince blinked hard, almost alarmed at where his mind had been going.

Laid by a *girl.* An *adult woman.* Jesus, Trey was just a kid.

No, he's twenty-two at least. He might even be older. And really, if you think about it, he's as pretty as most girls...

"You come back more often," Frank said, interrupting Vince's thoughts. "And you think about what I said. I know you've had your troubles with the women, and I know you don't want to get married again. But that doesn't mean you need to go live like a monk up on LaSalle. We don't need another Hank, hiding out and being gloomy. Come back to us, Vinnie. Come back to your family, where you belong."

Vince watched Trey Giles's sandy-blond hair fall as he bent his head and laughed at something someone at his table had said. "I'll come by more often, Uncle Frank." Vince's gaze stayed on Trey's hair. "I promise."

Chapter Three

Whoever came up with the idea of group projects, may he die a slow and torturous death.

It was hard enough balancing two jobs with my classes, and now the one night I wasn't waiting tables, I had to spend with five of my "peers". Never mind that I was older than all of them, albeit by only a few years. Never mind that their spoiled rich-kid attitudes rubbed me wrong. Never mind they couldn't remember my name: one called me Todd, the other called me *Hey you*—what was so hard about Trey?

The cold, hard truth was my grade now depended on five fuckwits. I wasn't about to let them ruin my GPA.

On some level I'd known it was a mistake, bringing them to Emilio's. I'd managed to talk them out of the first place they named—a tapas and wine bar that would have cost a fortune and left me hungry. The food at Emilio's was good and inexpensive, and the Fierros had always treated my Gram and me like family. The fact that the fuckwits had now apparently pissed off that family was like a rotten cherry on top of an already bad day. I could still feel Vinnie's piercing gaze on the back of my head.

I'd been trying to corral the rest of them into actually working for half an hour, to no avail. The two girls were too busy talking about the latest episode of *American Idol*, and the guys were too busy trying to impress the girls. I was about to ask for at least the third time if any of them had started their parts of the project yet, but one of the girls—Kat—cut me off.

"Did you guys register for fall semester yet?"

"I did," Ken said. "I got it down perfect. Nothing before noon, and no classes on Fridays."

"I don't mind morning classes," Kat replied. "It's the evening labs I hate. Don't they know we have lives?"

"I'm only taking twelve credits." Misty smiled at us as if she was giving us the answer to the meaning of life. "Any more than that is just too hard."

"Twelve is a lot if you have to work full-time too," I said, trying to be sympathetic.

She blinked at me, wrinkling her nose in confusion. She flicked her earring with a perfectly manicured nail, and I realized the absurdity of my assumption. She didn't work. Certainly she didn't work full-time.

"I registered for twenty-five credits." That was Aiden. He had the role of Entitled Youth down pat.

"Twenty-five?" I asked. "How can you do so much?"

He rolled his eyes. "I'm not going to keep them all. I sent the confirmation off to my dad. Now I just have to wait for the check. After I cash it, I'll drop most of them."

"Aiden, that's awful!" Kat laughed.

He shrugged. "As long as I keep one class, I'm good. I'll tell him I failed out, or that they interfered with my work schedule."

I looked down at my lap to hide my expression. It wouldn't do to have them see how much I hated them. How much I resented them all, cashing their daddies' checks, living in apartments they didn't have to pay for, not even bothering to appreciate what they had. I worked over fifty hours most weeks. Thirty-four at the restaurant, the most they'd give me, because even one more would require them to give me benefits, and they were too cheap for that. Thirty-four hours of screaming chefs and bitchy patrons, all for the lousy tips that would pay the bills and Gram's second mortgage. Then I worked another fifteen hours at the coffee shop, rising at 4:40 so I could be there when they opened at 5:00, burning my hands on steamed milk and skinny half-cafs just so I could afford one class a semester. If I was lucky, I'd earn my degree in another year and a half. That was *if* my mother didn't go on another spending binge or Gram didn't break her hip. If there were no household problems, like the broken pipe that flooded our small basement and stole my class from me three semesters ago.

They paused in their exchange of Tales of Beating the System, and I did my best to reroute them back to the task at hand. For better or for worse, forty-five minutes later we stopped working—Aiden was bored, Kat didn't have enough money in her meter and Misty had a headache. Of course they all promised to get their part done the very next day, but I'd learned long ago exactly how much a promise meant: absolutely fucking nothing.

It was just as well that we wrapped things up though because I wanted to check in with Gram before I headed off to The Rose for my shift. I owed her that, and a whole lot more.

My dad died shortly after my second birthday. He was shot during what should have been a routine traffic stop. I didn't even have a memory of him to console me. So many times, I'd pored over the photos of us at our old house in Oak Park, my dad pushing me on a baby swing, or laughing while I stood wearing his badge, his police cap hanging down over my eyes. I'd tried to convince myself that I remembered him, but I was old enough now to admit the truth. He was nothing more than a shadow in my mind where happiness should have been.

Two years after his death, we'd come to live with his parents. I hadn't understood why. Back then, I'd loved Gram's narrow brownstone on Loomis: my grandfather had still been alive, and I'd come home from school to see him fussing with our tiny spec of yard in an eternal battle with the shade trees before his shift at the plant, or touching up the paint on the rail. The neighborhood had been full of kids, many of them Fierros, and our house was warm with laughter and love.

Now our section of the block was more than a little

rundown, and Gram's brownstone wasn't helping anything. Even if any of us had time to touch up the paint on the railing, we wouldn't waste money on it. The steps had finally become so rickety we'd had to deal with them, but that had amounted to me clumsily nailing thicker boards over the top of the broken ones and hoping no inspector came by to tell me I was breaking city code. The yard was a weedy, barren mess. The neighborhood mostly housed college students. There were no packs of kids running the streets. No kickball games. No Kick the Can. And as for our house—well, I loved my Gram and my mom, but the laughter had stopped long ago.

"Gram," I called when I came in the front door. "I'm home. Did you need me to go to the store for anything before I go to work?"

It wasn't Gram who answered though. It was my mom's voice that drifted in from the kitchen.

"I already went to the store. I'm making your favorite: goulash."

Goulash hadn't been my favorite since I'd hit puberty and learned to distinguish Chef Boyardee from dog food. "I won't be here for dinner. I have to work tonight."

My mom came out of the kitchen with her paring knife still clutched in her right hand. She wore jeans and T-shirt, and she even had on a bit of makeup. She looked better than she had in a long time, though she did have a needy look about her that set off the old alarm bells. "But, honey, I was all set to make you dinner then take you to a movie."

Why exactly she'd decided out of the blue to try to turn the evening into a mother/son date was anyone's guess. "I can't. Not tonight."

"But, Trey—"

"I have to work, Ma. What do you want me to do? Call in sick?"

Even suggesting such a thing was a mistake. "You could.

Then we could go—"

"I was kidding."

Her smile disappeared. Her shoulders drooped. She sighed, a big dramatic gesture full of self-pity, because although it was me working two jobs while trying to go to school, in her mind she was the one who was really being inconvenienced. "I get so lonely. You're never here, and Gram isn't much company. I don't know anybody—"

"We've lived here for more than twenty years. You know everybody."

"But I don't have any friends."

We'd been over this, more times than I could count. They say misery loves company, but the truth is, misery gets lonely pretty damn fast. "Mom, I don't have time for this right now."

"You never have time. You work too hard. You should be home—"

I turned away, heading up the stairs to change into my work clothes. What could I say to her? Yes, I was young. Yes, life was unfair. I would have loved to be one of the college boys who could show up to a few classes and spend the rest of my time getting high. But the fact of the matter was, somebody had to pay the mortgage.

It wasn't going to be Mom.

"Don't wait up," I said. I didn't bother to acknowledge the disappointment on her face. God knew she'd never bothered to acknowledge mine.

Chapter Four

A few nights after he'd gone to Emilio's, Vince called his sister Rachel. She answered on the third ring.

"Vinnie. I thought you'd forgotten my phone number."

"Hey, Rach. Sorry. Been busy." He rubbed hard against the back of his neck. "What about you? Are you busy? Right now, I mean?"

Rachel went immediately serious. "I knew it. Something's wrong, isn't it. You never call unless something's wrong."

"Nothing's wrong," Vince lied. "I just wondered if I could stop by and talk to you, that's all."

"Sure, hon. Where are you?"

That was a good question. Vince looked around to get his bearings. "Rush and Wabash."

"Okay. See you soon."

It was past ten when Vinnie finally got to Rachel's apartment. She lived in the Marina Towers, three floors from the top, which Vinnie hated because he always felt like he was going to puke from the wind-resistant design. The term was a not-so-humorous oxymoron, because while the building might be safer from damage, "wind resistant" for the residents meant a great deal of swaying back and forth. Normally he got used to it once he'd been in the building for awhile, or once he'd had a few drinks, but when the wind was up like it was tonight, the motion never seemed to subside, which was why he had to stop halfway down her hallway and let the wall prop him up for a minute before he continued on to her door.

She answered wearing what he would have sworn was a bright blue kimono over a soft peach lacy number with spaghetti straps. Vince staggered back a few steps and held up his hands. "What the hell, Rach?"

"What?" Frowning, she glanced down at herself before rolling her eyes. "Jesus, Vinnie. You think I'm supposed to get dressed because my big lunk of a brother is coming over?"

"You trying to tell me you were sitting around the house wearing that?" he demanded.

Now she was mad. "If I'd known you were coming over to play Italian Big Brother, I would have told you to stay home. I was getting ready for bed, if you must know. Are you coming in or what?"

Vince grunted and shoved his hands in his pockets, keeping them there as she pulled the door open wider and he shuffled inside.

Rachel's apartment was the same as it ever was: like an ad out of some luxury-living magazine. Like the ones, in fact, that she'd pored over as a kid when she'd hid out in his bedroom. Everything was sleek and white and minimal and arranged to take in the amazing view of Lake Michigan through the open curtains. Vince hated it, because he always felt like he was going to get something dirty. Which was why he didn't sit down on the couch but sat on one of the chrome barstools and watched Rachel pull down the bottle of Oban and pour him three fingers into a tumbler.

"You should be nicer to me, considering what I picked up this afternoon." She slid the glass toward Vince, then opened a cupboard as he took the first sip of scotch. The woodsy smoke taste exploded over his tongue, making him wish he'd brought a cigar—and then he saw she'd produced a box of Havana Ovals and a lighter.

Groaning, Vince sagged against the bar and held out his hand. When she only lifted her eyebrows and smirked at him, he said, "Please, Rach. I'm sorry I freaked out that you met me at the door like a streetwalker."

She snorted, but she smiled too, and most importantly she passed the cigarettes over. Vince was a bit of a snob when it came to cigarettes—he only smoked Nat Shermans, usually settling for the naturals. Havana Ovals weren't made with Havana tobacco anymore, but they were the Cadillacs of the Nat Sherman line: rich, unfiltered 100s wrapped in brown paper. Vince drew the box to his nose, shut his eyes and inhaled. It smelled like tobacco and heaven.

"Take them out to the balcony," she called over her shoulder as she poured gin into her martini shaker.

Vince grabbed his scotch and tucked the cigarettes and lighter into his pocket before weaving his way carefully through the living room to the double doors off the dining area that led to the balcony. The breeze coming off the lake was a wind up this high, but he didn't mind. He felt the sway out here too, but for some reason it never bothered him outside as much. Something to do with physics, he supposed. He stood a minute holding his scotch, his other hand in his pocket, and he took in the glorious night. Sighing happily, he set the glass on the bistro table, pulled out the Havana Ovals and tucked himself into a corner to light up. He always smoked Nats, but the Ovals had no filter, which meant a moment of adjustment as he tried not to get the raw tobacco on his tongue. Eventually he got it lit and tossed the box and lighter onto the table next to his drink. Vince leaned against the iron rail and savored his cigarette.

Rachel came up beside him, martini glass in her hand. Vince passed over his cigarette before she could ask for it and went to the corner to light himself a new one as he returned to the rail. They stood there for several minutes drinking and smoking in silence as they watched the lights of the city play below until they were swallowed up beside the darkness of the lake.

Rachel ashed over the edge. "So what's eating you, big

brother?"

Vince cradled his scotch in the center of his palm and trailed a car down Lake Shore Drive. "It's complicated."

Rachel didn't say anything, just waited, letting Vince take his time.

Which was why he had come to her. Even if he thought he could have discussed this with anyone else in his family, he still would have come to Rachel, because everyone else would have talked him to death. Everyone else would have used the lag it took him to get started to talk about themselves. Most of the time that didn't bother him. He liked listening to his family. He liked it, mostly, when they meddled. But this was too complicated for that. So he stood there with Rachel, drinking and smoking until both their cigarettes were spent and their glasses were empty, and about ten minutes after that he cleared his throat and said, "I've kind of been thinking that maybe"— his heart clenched, and he shut his eyes—"I've been thinking that maybe I—"

But he couldn't say it. *I think I might be a little bit queer.* It was terrifying enough in his head, but not even Oban and Havana Ovals and the view from Rachel's balcony helped him get the words out.

Rachel's hand landed on his shoulder and massaged gently. "You want some more scotch, hon?"

Yes, he did, but Vince wasn't sure he could keep it down with the way his stomach was dancing. He shook his head.

Rachel's massage ended with an encouraging squeeze. "Just take your time, Vinnie."

Vince nodded and trained his eyes on Lake Shore, willing the traffic to hypnotize him. It did, a little, lulling his panic back to a dull roar, and he decided to try a different approach. "There was this call the other day. Down in Lakeview. I took it because everyone was out and it sounded like a pretty simple leaky disposal." The story relaxed him further, and his grip on the rails eased. "It was these two guys. They both met me at the door and were real nice, thanking me for coming so quickly, and then one of them went back into the den and the other guy took me to the kitchen. They were regular guys. I mean, at first I figured they were roommates or something. They had the game on in the other room, for God's sake. They were just guys." He paused for a breath. "But then I saw this picture. It was the two of them, sitting all close together like a portrait, like a couple, and that's when I realized it. They were gay. And—" He stopped, hitting the wall again.

Rachel waited for half a minute before replying. "Vinnie, are you telling me..." She trailed off, not finishing.

Vince gripped the rails until his knuckles were white. "No. I mean, I don't think so." He sighed and sagged forward. "Hell, Rach. I don't know what I mean. All I know is that I've felt weird ever since then. All messed up. The way I heard them talking from the other room. I don't know. It doesn't make any sense at all, but I keep thinking..." He pushed off the rail and turned away, grabbing the box of cigarettes.

He took his time lighting up, lingering a little in the corner, bracing his arm above his head against the wall as he tried to collect himself. He didn't notice Rachel leave the balcony, but she must have because when she nudged his arm, she was handing him his refilled glass of scotch, and when he turned back around to sip it, he saw the bottle sitting on the table.

She leaned against the door, idly trying to light her own cigarette. When Vince tried to take the lighter to do it for her, she waved him off and motioned to his drink. He sipped at it, watching her.

"I mean, I'm not," he said, not exactly sure it was true, but feeling better for saying so. "I played around when I was at school, but it didn't mean anything."

"You're telling me you had sex with guys in college?"

Vince nearly dropped his scotch. "No." He set the drink

down, took a heavy toke on the Havana Oval and grabbed the lighter from Rachel, cupping his hand around it as he sparked the flame for her. "No, not 'guys'. *Guy*. One. And it wasn't sex. It was just playing, like I said."

Rachel inhaled, lowered the cigarette and blew smoke out of the corner of her mouth. "What's playing? Are you talking hand jobs, or blowjobs, or what?"

Vince retreated back to his corner and kept his eyes on the floor of the balcony. "Both. I mean, I never gave one," he added quickly. That had always seemed so important, and it was a lifeline right now. "But there was this guy. We'd jerk each other off a lot, and..." he reached for his scotch and took a deep drink, "...sometimes he'd blow me. But it was just fucking around. I think he was gay, but...you know."

Daring a glance at Rachel, he saw that no, she didn't know. She didn't look disgusted, but she did look confused. "I don't get it. He was gay, but you were...what?"

I don't know. "Horny." He drew again on the cigarette. Then he shrugged. "He wanted me to fuck him. I didn't want to. That was too far. *That* was gay." He ashed out and glared at the floor. "I wasn't gay. I dated girls, Rach."

"But you played around with a gay man." When Vince started to panic again, she held up a hand. "I'm trying to understand, sweetie."

So was Vince. He let his head fall back against the wall. "I mean, hell. I don't have any idea how many women I've dated." Panic swelled, terror racing up from his feet like a fire. Bolstered by high-quality scotch and Nat Sherman's finest tobacco, he made himself say the rest. "But I've always noticed guys too."

He felt like he'd jumped over the rail of Rachel's balcony. For the first time in his life, he wished she weren't as one with silence as he was, wished she had their mother's penchant for filling spaces with questions and observations. Rachel was quiet a long time, so he made himself wait, and breathe.

The scotch and the Havanas helped.

"Okay," Rachel said at last. "Here's what I need help with. Are you telling me that you like women *and* men, and that's what you realized when you were at this couple's house, or are you telling me that you like men and have all along but liked women enough that you could fake it and don't want to anymore?"

Vince felt dizzy. Almost sick. Because that was the question, wasn't it? He'd been telling himself he was trying to work out if this was some stupid...phase? Crazy idea? Psychosis? Something along those lines. But leave it to Rach to skip right over that and into the belly of the beast.

"I don't know," he whispered at last.

He wanted her to come over and hug him. To ruffle his hair and tease him and call him silly and promise him it would all be okay. To reassure him that he wasn't... Hell. He didn't even know the word for it. Messed up. Delusional.

Wrong in the eyes of God and his family.

She didn't, though. She wasn't forming the sign of the cross with her fingers and backing away, but she was quiet and thoughtful, not comforting. "Well," she said at last, "I have to say, I didn't see this coming."

Vince couldn't take it anymore. "Rach," he whispered.

Thank God, thank *God*, she did come over to him then, extinguishing her Havana in the silver ashtray she kept on the sill before she took him in her arms, making gentle shushing noises as she stroked his hair and kissed the side of his ear. "It's okay, baby," she promised softly. "You're okay. Straight, bi, gay—I'm going to love you no matter what you are, forever."

Her words were a relief and a terror at once. "I'm not gay," he objected, his voice rough.

She kissed him again, on his temple this time. "You might be, hon. And don't freak out like that. I know this has to break every piece of the Italian macho code they programmed into your DNA, but let me be the first to inform you that gay men can be pretty macho too."

"But I don't *know* that I'm—that," Vince insisted. He sounded a little whiny, he knew, but Jesus. Not *that*.

To his surprise, Rachel got angry. "Gay, Vincent. You can say it without bursting into flames. Gay. G-A-Y gay." She reached for his scotch and drained the last of it. "You insult half my advertising team when you act like it's a disease instead of an orientation. And let me promise you, if you persist in thinking gay equals effeminate, I'm going to have Steven show up at your apartment in his leather gear and Dom your ass into next week."

Vince had no idea what she was talking about, but he got the message loud and clear. He nodded curtly. "I don't mean to disrespect your friends," he said, and he meant it. "It's just hard for me, Rach. And I don't *know* what I am. I really don't." He crossed to the bottle of Oban, took his glass back from her and poured liberally. "But hell, what if that's been the problem all this time, why I can't stay with a woman?"

Rachel snorted. "You can't stay with a brand of shampoo, Vinnie. You have commitment issues that have commitment issues."

Vince ignored that. Because he'd gotten a lot of mileage out of this idea, that maybe the problem wasn't the girl but that she wasn't a guy. Scary as that was, it wasn't anything compared to the idea that he wasn't an ass, he was just barking up the wrong tree. Well, it wasn't scary until he sat with it for a few minutes too long. "What if it made the difference, Rach?"

She pursed her lips and held up her hand. "Back up, Vinnie. Back way up. Two minutes ago you couldn't say 'gay', and don't think it hasn't escaped me that you can't say the word, but now dating a man might change your whole life?"

Well, put like that, it did sound bad. Vince sighed.

"And don't do that either," she went on. "Don't go giving up before you start. You know, you might be partly right. This could be the way to go for you. At the very least you might not propose on the second date for a change because you're so sure rainbows will start flying out of your ass." Rachel reached out and rubbed his shoulder. "How about you explore this? How about you go check out a gay bar sometime and see?"

Vince thought about it a moment, then nodded. It did make a kind of sense. He could check it out. Go into a bar where no one would know him and see. See if it clicked. See if it felt like coming home or going to hell. See if he flirted with men as well as he flirted with women. He swallowed hard. Okay, maybe he wouldn't even flirt the first time. But Rachel was right. He could go check things out.

Clutching his scotch tightly, he nodded.

Rachel smiled and turned her gentle stroking of his shoulder into a soft punch. "There you go. See? It's going to be okay, Vinnie. One way or another. I promise."

Vince nodded again. *It's all going to be okay.*

Jesus, he hoped so.

Chapter Five

The club scene wasn't exactly my speed, but we all have to make sacrifices.

I had three best friends, and we tried to take turns calling the shots. Last weekend had been World of Warcraft, because Josh and Tara loved to play. Dillon and I made the best of it. Friday night, they'd all followed me downtown for a midnight showing of an action film, even though they hated it. Tonight we were at After Hours, mostly because Dillon wanted to get laid.

It's not like I can't dance, or like I'm too much of a prude to drink, but the club Dillon picked was a pure meat market. Every guy there was cruising.

Every guy but me, I guess.

Next to me, Tara and Josh had their heads together and were talking about something—probably gaming. They're straight, and I'm pretty sure they're crazy about each other, but they recite the "just friends" line like it's the fucking gospel. Who am I to argue? Out on the dance floor, Dillon was practically swallowing some guy's tongue.

I checked my watch. Only eleven o'clock. If we were lucky, Dillon would decide to cut to the chase and leave with the guy soon, and Tara, Josh and I would be off the hook. But I doubted that was going to happen.

"I'm going to get a drink," I said to them. I probably should have offered to bring one back, but Josh already owed me too much money.

I fought my way through the crowd, doing my best not to

make eye contact. Sometimes, that seemed to be all it took for some guy to think I was issuing an invitation. Still, I could feel their eyes on me. I saw the way a couple turned to watch me pass.

"Hey, sweet thing," one said. "Let me buy you a drink."

I ignored him and kept walking.

I finally made it to the bar. "Coke, please." The bartender stared at me like they always do when you don't order alcohol—like I'm some kind of idiot. "Just a Coke, please," I said again. He managed to avoid rolling his eyes at me, but not by much. He pulled out a glass and started shoveling in ice. If they're nice about it, I tip them. If they give me the soda for free, I tip them. But he charged me and was a dick to boot, so I didn't bother.

I was just turning to head back to our table when I spotted him: dark hair, dark skin, sitting on the barstool looking so out of place, I wondered how I hadn't seen him before.

"Vinnie?" I yelled, moving around the barflies in between us to get to him. "Vincent Fierro, is that you?"

What a stupid fucking question. Of course it was him. And when he turned to me, the blood drained from his face like I was the goddamn ghost of Christmas past. "Trey," he said. "What are you doing here?"

Well, at least we were tied on the stupid-question front. There wasn't an empty stool next to him, so I angled myself into the narrow space between him and the bar. "I've never seen you here before."

"It's my first time."

"I didn't realize you were gay."

All the color that had left his cheeks came back with a vengeance. The glare he turned on me would have made me back up, if I'd had anywhere to go. "I'm not."

I laughed. What the hell else could I do? "Oh yeah? Let me guess. You wandered in here by mistake, saw all the guys practically having sex on the dance floor, and thought you'd just pull up a seat for the hell of it, right? 'Cause that's what all the straight guys do."

He clenched his jaw, turning away from me, and I felt a twinge of guilt for having goaded him. Big tough guy like him, big Catholic family, it couldn't be as easy for him as it had been for me. My Gram had barely batted an eye when I'd come out to her, and that had been six years ago.

"It's cool, Vinnie," I said. "I get it."

He seemed uncertain, and I did my best to be reassuring. "Let me buy you a drink."

He winced, glancing around the bar like he was searching for an escape hatch. "I don't think I'm staying."

Christ, offer to buy a guy a drink, and he's ready to bolt. He probably assumed I was trying to get in his pants. Of course, I'd been in that position a billion times myself, so I didn't take it personally. "You don't have to go. I'll leave you alone—"

"No!" I had a feeling the word had escaped without him meaning for it to. He looked like he regretted it. I wasn't sure what to say. I wasn't sure if assuring him that I wasn't cruising was what he wanted to hear or not.

He took a deep breath and blew it out. "I didn't mean because of you," he said at last. "I just mean, I really hate this scene. What the hell kind of music is this anyway?"

"Club music."

"I keep wondering if this goddamn song will ever end. It's been going on for at least an hour."

I laughed. "No, it hasn't. This is some club mashup of 'Umbrella' and 'Single Ladies'. That last song was something by Lady Gaga. The one before I think was—"

"You mean these are *real songs*?"

I laughed. "What else would they be?"

He rolled his eyes. "I thought it was a techno loop clubs played when they couldn't afford to hire a real DJ. Or a band. I didn't realize people actually *listened* to this shit." He shook his head, rubbing his forehead with his fingers. "Fuck, I'm old."

The music wasn't exactly my speed either, although I'd long since grown immune to it. "What kind of music do you like?" I asked.

"Jazz. Swing. *Real* music. Three notes by Coltrane, and this crap would back off in shame."

His answer gave me an idea that was too good to pass up. "Come on. Let's get out of here."

The look he gave me was almost like panic, and I smiled. "I don't mean, 'your place or mine?' I just mean, let's go someplace better."

"Where?" he asked, looking relieved.

"Trust me."

I took a minute to pull out my phone and send a text to Tara. *Leaving. Be safe.*

Her *WTF?* came back to me in record time—I'd never left the club with anybody before—but I ignored it.

I led him out of the hot, loud club into the cool night air. The sidewalks were still wet, but the rain had stopped. The only part of the music we could hear from outside was the thumping bass. My ears were ringing. "You mind walking?" I felt like my voice was way too loud.

"I don't mind."

We rounded the corner and went a few blocks. "You know where you're going?" he asked as we walked.

"Of course. I've never been in this club before, but I've heard about it."

We reached our destination. No thumping bass here. I opened the door, and smooth jazz flowed out around us, wrapping us up, drawing us in.

Inside, the lights were low—no bright lights or flashing strobes. A few couples were dancing. A lone black man sat on a stool in the corner, playing a sax. The music was sultry, loud enough to be heard, but not so loud you couldn't hear the person four inches away from you.

I glanced over at Vinnie, and he smiled. His smile was cute. Sort of smartass and self-deprecating at the same time—like he was daring the world to take him seriously. It made him seem years younger.

"Better," he said.

We found a table near the dance floor, and the waiter didn't bat an eye when I only ordered a Coke. Vinnie ordered a vodka tonic, and then we sat there, not knowing what to say. When I realized he would wait until doomsday before breaking the ice, I fished around until I found something that felt safe to talk about. "Sorry about the idiots in the restaurant the other day. I made them tip Marcie well."

It was a little astounding how much this subject relaxed him, and I can't say I minded the look of approval I got either. "They didn't seem like your usuals." His tone hinted heavily that I generally had more taste.

"Group project," I explained.

He made a face and shook his head. "They're still doing that shit? I figured they'd quit once they saw what a mess it was."

"Are you kidding? A week's worth of group project is that much less shit for professors to grade. Plus they get to say they're teaching us team building and crap like that."

Vinnie rolled his eyes. "Whatever. Well, you have my condolences."

He tipped his glass toward mine, and I met him in a toast. We drank, our gazes tangled in a moment of camaraderie. I didn't want it to end, so I gave him another conversation prompt. "What is it you do? I know you don't work for the restaurant anymore, because they're always carrying on about how 'If Vinnie was here, this wouldn't have happened.'"

He raised a dubious eyebrow into his hairline. "That I didn't know. This recent, this carrying on?"

I tried to think. "Yeah, I think so. Last week was the last time it came up."

He grimaced. "They're probably getting ready to gang up on me again to come back. Thanks for the intel."

"But what is it you do now?"

"Plumbing." He took a drink. "I work for my uncle up in Northbrook. Parino Brothers Plumbing." I tried not to be shocked, but I must have failed because he laughed and waggled both eyebrows. "Hey, somebody's got to unclog the toilets."

"But do you *like* that?" I pressed. It was probably rude, but I knew he'd gone to not just college but graduate school, that he had an MBA and used to do accounting for his family's restaurants. Now he fished out drains?

He shrugged. "It's okay. Pay's good, and I get out and about." He gave me a sideways smile that made my stomach turn over. "Haven't you heard my family gossiping about how I'm the one who can't settle down on anything?"

I had. Vince always had a new job, and he'd been married three times, unless I'd missed an ex-wife in there. "Whatever makes you happy, I guess."

This comment made his smile die, and he became focused on turning his drink casually in his hand. "Not sure about that. Do my best, though." Clearing his throat, he set his glass down. "What about you? You're in school, right? What for?"

"English major. I originally wanted to be pre-law, but at the rate I'm having to go, I'll be ninety when I get out. I thought about getting an education endorsement, though my advisor is trying to talk me into political science." I shrugged and twirled the straw in my Coke. "Right now I'll be happy to get far enough into a degree to be able to graduate. I'm tired of school."

Vinnie frowned at me. "How old are you, if you don't mind my asking?"

"Twenty-five. And yes, I know it's a long time to be in school."

To my surprise, Vinnie only nodded. "You're taking care of your grandmother and mother, though, and you work full-time, right?"

"More than. I have two jobs. Barista at Full Moon, the coffee shop up on Racine just north of the interstate, and waiter at The Rose." I was ready for his look of disdain, and I had to bite back a smile. "Hey, we can't all be born into the Fierro clan."

"Have you ever applied at Emilio's, though?"

"When I was looking, there wasn't an opening. Plus, I hate to be rude, but the tips are higher at The Rose. All those lovely tourists coming out of the Loop, grateful to get a table."

"The food's terrible. They only survive because that bastard has city councilors in his pocket." He ironed out his scowl and held up a hand in surrender. "But you're right. The tips have to be killer."

"If it helps, the chef's an ass. Mostly because I won't blow him in the back room, I'm pretty sure." Too late I realized I'd accidentally shined a spotlight on the elephant in the middle of our table. I winced. Vinnie slouched and took a heavy hit from his drink. He wouldn't look me in the eye anymore, and it made me sad.

This time, though, it was Vinnie who brought us back into conversation. "So you come up here a lot?"

"To Boystown? Not often if I can help it. Don't get me wrong. It's a great neighborhood, but mostly I see the bars, which I could do without." This got me the eyebrow again, and another one of those sexy little smiles. "What?" I demanded, trying to tamp down the butterflies that smile unleashed in my belly.

"You're young. You're cute. Yet you could do without going to bars full of guys wanting to hook up with you?"

He thought I was cute? My butterflies went crazy, and I focused all my attention on my drink. "I feel like I should tell you something." I concentrated on trying to spear my thin red cocktail straw through one of the round ice cubes in my Coke, debating how to tell him I was a virgin. "I don't have sex."

"What?" Vinnie asked, laughing. "Not ever?"

I glanced up at him, trying not to be bothered by the amused disbelief in his eyes. "I just mean, I don't sleep with guys on the first date."

His laughter died fast. "This isn't a date."

He said it like a threat, as if he had to set the record straight—and I do mean *straight*—and I laughed. His protests actually took a great deal of pressure off me. "All the more reason I won't sleep with you tonight."

I was glad when he smiled again. "Deal," he said.

It was strange how freeing that word was.

I'd learned over the years to be so careful about my interactions with men, lest they misunderstand my intentions, but it wasn't as if I was opposed to sex or to fooling around. I wasn't immune to the calling of my own hormones. I woke up horny like any healthy male. The problem was that with most guys, the line between flirting and fucking was razor thin. But Vince wasn't most guys. He wasn't some stranger I'd barely met. I'd known him for most of my life. I knew I could trust him.

Suddenly, I felt I could throw caution to the wind. Having the boundaries firmly in place and a partner I trusted opened up the playing field considerably.

I reached over and put my hand on his thigh, and he raised one eyebrow questioningly at me. "No sex," I said, "but that doesn't mean we can't flirt, right?"

He stared hard at me for a long second, like I was some bridge he couldn't decide if he wanted to jump off of. Eventually he said, his voice low and rough, "I guess not."

My heart went into overdrive. It made me bold. It was a new

feeling for me, and I embraced it. I had nothing to lose.

I moved into his lap, straddling his thighs so I could face him. His hands were on my legs, but it wasn't as if he was touching me on purpose. It was more like that was the safest place he could find to put them. His guards were back up in full. "This doesn't feel like flirting."

"Then what does it feel like?"

"Like you're coming on to me." He said the words like an accusation.

"Aren't they same thing?" He didn't move as I undid the top button on his shirt. "We already said no sex." I undid the next one. "Relax." There wasn't much hair on his chest. Just smooth, dark skin, and I caressed it with my fingertips. I traced his collarbone. I put my arms around his neck and leaned closer to kiss his cheek, which was stubbly, and then the side of his neck. "God, you smell good." It was a spicy scent—some kind of aftershave—mixed with the clean, soapy smell of his hair. I kissed him again, below his ear, and I heard his breath catch in his throat.

He clenched his hands. His fingers dug into my thigh. "Trey—"

I knew he was going to tell me to stop, and I cut him off, leaning back a bit so I could look in his eyes. "Dance with me."

The request surprised him, and his eyebrows went up. "Are you serious?"

"Of course." I eyed the couples on the floor—it was nothing like the club scene. The couples here were arm in arm, cheek to cheek, some of them talking quietly, some of them kissing, all of them looking like they were in love. I envied them. They were a mix of orientations too, which I hoped would calm him.

I turned back to Vinnie. "Nobody's ever danced with me like this before."

"But we're both guys."

I laughed. "No kidding."

It took him a second to react. Maybe he was deciding whether or not to be offended, but then he smiled. "I guess."

I resisted the urge to clap like a silly kid, even though I wanted to. I stood up, and he let me take his hand and lead him to the dance floor. I led him to an empty space between the swaying couples and turned to face him.

"This is weird," he said.

"No, it's not." I stepped closer, sliding my left hand around his waist as I put my right hand in his. "I assume you want to lead?"

"That's what I'm used to." He put his arm around me, although he didn't hold me close. It was like those dances in junior high, where you were supposed to keep six inches of open space between you and your partner. "Your left hand is supposed to be on my shoulder."

"Says who?" Before he could answer, I closed the distance between us. I put my head on his shoulder, my nose against his neck so I could smell his aftershave. "Quit being an uptight prick and dance with me."

He made an angry noise low in his throat, almost like he was growling at me, but he didn't pull away, and we started to move.

The dancing part turned out to be easy. The part about not being uptight took a bit longer, but by the time the next song began, he was doing better. He stopped being so stiff, and more importantly he didn't pull away when I tightened my arm around him and melted into him. I shut my eyes and let myself go. His body was so strong and solid against mine. I could feel him breathing. He was taller then me, and when he turned his head toward me, his warm breath tickled my ear. His hand moved slowly up and down my back as we swayed.

How many times had I wondered how it would feel to have a man hold me like this? It was wonderful. I thought I might be in heaven. I held him tighter, concentrating on how close his lips were to my ear. I wished he would kiss me there, just once. I slid my left hand out from behind him, up his chest and around his neck. I tangled my fingers into his thick black hair. I tilted my head back, urging his head down a bit, guiding his lips to the wonderfully sensitive flesh below my ear.

He didn't kiss me, but his breathing became heavier. He held me against him. He had an erection. The bulge in his pants pushed against my groin.

Any blood that might have been in my brain fled quickly to parts further south.

"Oh Jesus," he moaned, and suddenly he was trying to jerk away from me. "I need to go."

I held on to him though, refusing to let him bolt. I tilted my head back to look up at him. I could see something like panic on his face, although he wouldn't actually meet my eyes. He seemed to be looking everywhere else.

"No you don't. Dance with me some more."

He finally met my eyes, and even in the low light, I could see the color rising on his cheeks. "I can't..."

"We're just dancing."

"It doesn't feel like 'just dancing' anymore."

I almost laughed. Almost. "There's nothing wrong with being turned on. There's nothing wrong with what we're feeling." My words clearly embarrassed him more, and this time I really did laugh. I couldn't believe I had to tell a guy more than ten years my senior that it was okay to have a boner. I tightened my left arm around his neck. I didn't so much pull him down as I used my arm around his neck to pull myself up, so we were nose to nose, forehead to forehead, our lips almost touching. "Dancing feels good, Vin. Being close like this feels good. Why do we have to be embarrassed about that?"

I thought for a second he was going to pull away. He was looking into my eyes, as if he couldn't decide whether to believe me or not, but he sighed, and some of the tension went out of him. "Okay."

He let me direct his head back down where it had been, so his warm breath bathed my neck. He let me push my erection against his. He held me tight against him.

We danced.

Admittedly, it probably wasn't much of a dance. I wasn't even sure we were still moving. It was more like we were in contest to see who could get closer to the other, like we were trying to occupy the very same tiny space on the floor. I wondered if he could feel the frantic beat of my heart. It felt like there was nothing but music holding us up. Song after song after song. I lost track of how many. The music was sexy and sultry, and if smoke had a sound, that would have been it. Vinnie never let me go, not even in those quiet seconds between songs. I lost myself in his smell, his hand caressing my back, his breath against my neck, his groin hard against mine.

We might have been the last two people in the bar, or in the whole wide world, and I wouldn't have noticed. My head was spinning, my groin aching, my body practically thrumming with the desire to feel him touch me more. I kissed his neck. His hand slid down my back, past my belt. He squeezed a little, and I whimpered.

"Oh Jesus," he whispered again, but he didn't pull away.

I'd laughed so many times at people who claimed sex "just happened," but for the first time in my life, I thought I understood. I wanted him so much. I didn't care that we were in public. I didn't care that I barely knew him. I only knew the pressure in my groin was the sweetest madness I'd ever felt. Knowing he was as turned on as I was made me breathless. I would have thrown my virginity away in a heartbeat, if he'd been willing to take it. It would have been easy for him to convince me to go home with him. I imagined being alone at his place, dancing as we were now, only without our clothes. Dancing to nothing but flickering candlelight.

"Trey," he whispered at last.

He pulled away a bit and looked down into my eyes. Had he changed his mind about the sex? Had I?

"I should go," he said.

I wasn't sure if I was disappointed or relieved. I wanted to keep dancing, but I knew we were asking for trouble. "I know."

It took us a minute to disentangle. If we'd let go too fast, I'm sure neither of us would have been able to stand. It was more like a slow transition from being one body back to being two. It made me sad, but it also made me aware of just how lost I'd really been.

He pulled his shirt out of his pants as we walked back to the table, letting it hang over his groin. I didn't bother. Nobody was paying any attention to us, and even if they were, I suspected we weren't the only guys in the place sporting wood.

My hand shook as I picked up my Coke and drained it. Vin was pointedly not making eye contact, but I saw him run his hand through his hair, and I was pretty sure he was shaking as much as I was. Somehow, that gave me confidence.

"Good thing this isn't a date," I said, and he smiled over at me.

I led him back out onto the street. The sidewalks were still damp. The air was still cool. Was this still the same night? Was it even my same life? I glanced down at my watch. It was almost three o'clock in the morning. We'd been in the bar for more than three hours? It seemed impossible.

I looked up to find him watching me. "You taking the EL?" he asked, nodding down the street toward the station.

"Yeah. Are you?"

"I drove."

He cleared his throat uncomfortably, and in the blink of an eye, it was *the moment*. The awkward fucking moment where nobody knows what to say, nobody knows what to do. Should we kiss? Should we shake hands? Should we just turn and walk away? I wanted him to kiss me, but I knew there was no way he would. I'd have to make the first move. I wasn't sure I had the courage. In the bar, with the lights down low and the music playing, it had been easy to flirt. But in the cold crisp air of night, with the streetlights looking on, I didn't think I could do it. I wondered how he'd react. I had a feeling it wouldn't please him.

"Well." He rocked back on his heels like he was getting ready to run for his life. "Good night."

I sighed, disappointed that I'd lost my chance. "Good night."

He started to walk away, and I called out before I knew what I was going to say. "Vinnie, wait!"

He stopped and turned toward me. Why the hell had I stopped him? Shit! He was waiting for me to speak, and I felt like an ass. I took a deep breath and said the first thing that came to me.

"Thanks for the dance."

He smiled at me—that goddamn cute smile, like the whole world could kiss his ass—and I kind of hated the way it made me so happy to have him point it my way. "See you around."

Chapter Six

It didn't hit Vince until he was halfway home what he had done. He wandered back to the lot where he'd parked, paid the attendant and meandered into the early morning traffic to make his way home. On LaSalle he got caught in traffic behind an accident, and rather than detour to a different route, he stayed with the glut of cars, using the time to process what had happened that night. He thought about how he'd gone to Boystown, gotten picked up in a club, gone to another club and danced with another guy.

With Trey Giles.

That hadn't been what freaked him out. What had made him double over his steering wheel was realizing that he'd liked it.

A lot. He didn't know when he'd been that turned on, in fact.

And he'd been with a guy.

With Trey Fucking Giles.

He'd gone to see if it would help him make sense of what he was feeling, but it had only left him more confused. It had been going so well until Trey had shown up. Rather, it had been going terribly, which he'd thought meant he wasn't gay, that this was some crazy idea he'd had like usual. Nobody had turned him on. Not really. No one had wanted him either, and he hadn't imagined several young things murmuring "old man" and "grandpa" as he passed. He'd planned on finishing his drink so he could say he'd well and truly tried—and then there was Trey.

Trey, and the jazz club, and the "just flirting" and the dancing, and the almost coming in his pants on the dance floor because holy shit, did Trey's hair smell good.

So he hadn't reacted at the first bar, not to a room full of sex-crazed men, but he *had* reacted to Trey. The thing was, he'd thought when he figured this out one way or another, he'd feel good. That he'd be gay or not gay, and he'd know, and he'd deal with it. Except now that he'd gone, he felt more confused than before. He felt...not sick, but...terrified. That was what he felt. Absolutely fucking terrified. Of what he couldn't quite tell. Of being gay? Except he didn't feel gay.

Of course, maybe gay felt different than he supposed, and that meant he was.

Except—*shit.*

He parked in his garage and began the four-block trek back to his building, his brain continuing to spin out into full-blown panic. By the time he got to the Marshall Hotel he was almost hyperventilating. He had to stop and rest his head against the Thai restaurant's basement window until a homeless man asked him if he was all right. Vince had tried to lie and say yes, but he could only gurgle, so he handed over a five instead and made himself keep going until he got to the courtyard of his building.

He sat there for awhile, staring out at the neat, newly planted rows of marigolds by the long-defunct fountain.

He wasn't gay. He'd know if he was, right? That was what he had gone to do. To go and see. And he didn't know. He hadn't gone to Boystown and felt like he'd gone home. He'd gone to Boystown and felt very fucking old.

Dancing with Trey had felt...good. But weird. Hot. It had made him feel like he was on fire, like every nerve ending in his body had turned on.

Shit. Shit, he *was* gay!

No, no, the terrified part of his brain argued back. *No. I'm just confused. Confused and—confused.*

Vince shut his eyes and slouched down on the bench.

Well, whatever it was, whatever it had been, it wasn't happening again. He'd gone to see what it was like, and it had been a disaster. Except for those parts where it had felt amazing. Mostly it had been a disaster, though.

Right?

Swearing under his breath, Vince rose from the bench and headed for the door. Disaster or not, he took solace in the fact that he only saw Trey at the restaurant, and even then not unless he got there early. The odds of them ever meeting again were slim to none. Anyway, the kid was probably off laughing with his buddies over what a case he'd been. It wasn't like Trey was going to be looking for a repeat of their—not date, but whatever it had been.

He refused to let himself think about what it meant that the idea of Trey laughing about their night together made him achingly sad.

Chapter Seven

A smart man would have stayed far, far away from the train wreck that was Vincent Fierro. I knew that. But my Gram always says, "Follow your heart." And what my heart wanted was Vin.

It wasn't that I loved the guy. After all, I barely knew him. But I couldn't get that night out of my head. I couldn't get *him* out of my head. I couldn't stop thinking about how good it felt to be in his arms, tight up against him, dancing. I couldn't forget the tickle of his breath against my neck, and the way his hand felt as he caressed my back.

More than anything though, I couldn't get over how fucking good it felt to be *free*. Free to flirt and touch and to be honest about what I wanted. It wasn't that I was a virgin because I was a prude, or because I thought sex was a sin. I was curious about sex. I woke up with a boner. I jacked off like any other guy. And I sure as hell wasn't a virgin because I couldn't get laid. On the contrary, sometimes I felt like I was constantly warding off attacks. But my Gram taught me that sex should be about love, and I think she's right.

I'd told plenty of guys over the years that sex wasn't an option, but none of them had ever taken it with as much grace as Vinnie had. Some guys decided as soon as the words were out of my mouth that they were wasting their time. They'd bail on the date in record time, never to be heard from again. Some guys took it as a challenge, and I'd spend the rest of the night fighting off advances. A few had said, "Sure, Trey, I understand." They'd allowed the rule to stand through the first date, and even the second. Only one of them had made it to a third.

Nothing beyond that, though. Not a single guy yet had thought it was worth putting a fourth date into a possible relationship if sex wasn't part of the deal. Sharing my body with somebody was a gift, and I wasn't about to give it away to some asshole who couldn't bother to appreciate it.

The problem was, I still wanted to flirt. I wanted to make out. I wanted to do all those things that people did, but it never worked. Even when I'd been with guys who claimed they understood, I'd had to be so careful, lest I hear that word that seemed to follow me everywhere I went: tease. As if there was no middle ground between friendship and fucking. As if I couldn't even touch them without inviting more. It was like living in a cage. Like having wings but never being able to stretch them out, let alone fly. I hated it.

Vinnie had been different. Vinnie had actually seemed *relieved* to hear I wouldn't sleep with him. I could flirt, and touch, and maybe make out a bit, and I wouldn't be expected to put out at the end of the night. At the time I'd been fixated on that, loving the novelty of it, but as I thought about it more, I realized his relief had been not out of respect for me, but because sleeping with me was too far for him right now. He was experimenting. He was confused. He was...

Well, he was in the fucking closet with a raging case of denial, was what he was, but I could deal with that.

The more I thought about it, the more I thought it might work. As long as our clothes stayed on, he'd be able to tell himself he was straight, right? And me?

Well, I knew it was stupid as hell to get involved with a closeted guy just because he wouldn't expect sex, and yet, who the hell else was going to take me to a jazz club, let me be close to him and hot for him and crazy about him, and yet *not* expect me to jump into bed with him when it was over? Who the hell else would let me see what it felt like to spread my wings?

55

Nobody.

That was why my heart wanted Vin. And the more I thought about him, the more determined I was to have him.

I started going by the restaurant every morning, waiting for the day I'd see him. Part of me hoped he'd be happy to see me. I imagined him looking at me, his face lighting up. Logically, though, I knew that probably wasn't the way it would be. I'd given him my number, and he'd never called, despite the fact he'd been as turned on at the club as I'd been. It was safe to assume he was going to be a bit weird. It also stood to reason that I'd have to do all the work.

It was another week before I actually got my chance. An insurance group from Des Moines had been in town for a convention, done well, and stopped by The Rose Saturday to celebrate. I got two hundred from that one table in tips alone, and the next morning I wanted to celebrate.

I found my mom and Gram in the living room, watching TV. I would have preferred to not have to invite my mother, but she was sitting right there, and Gram could see the excitement on my face.

"What has you smiling?" she asked.

"I made some great tips last night. How about we go celebrate?"

My mom suddenly perked up. "Celebrate?"

"Yeah. I thought we could go out for dinner. Gram and I can have a bit of wine—"

The interest disappeared, and she turned back to the TV. "Yeah, that sounds great. I can sit and watch you both drink without me."

A second of silence while Gram and I looked at each other, consulting in silence, trying to decide the best way to handle it. Gram decided to opt for appeasement. She smiled at Mindy.

"We don't need wine," Gram said. "It'll just make me sleepy anyway."

"Sure!" After all, it was Vinnie I was really after anyway. "We'll get dessert instead."

"I'm already too fat to wear most of my clothes."

"Oh, Mindy, don't be silly," Gram said. "You look fine."

Mom didn't answer right away. Gram and I sat there, waiting to see which way she'd go this time. There was a chance she'd snap out of it and make the best of things. A slim chance. I mentally crossed my fingers, but in the next moment, she dashed any hopes of making things easy on me.

"Not much of a celebration though, is it?" she griped. "I can't drink. I can't have dessert—"

"Then stay home," I snapped.

She blinked over at me. She actually had the nerve to look wounded, which only made me angrier.

"I don't want to stay here alone while you guys go out."

She couldn't stand that we might have fun, with or without her. I sighed. "Stop acting like a goddamn martyr. Gram and I are going. You can stay, or you can come with us. It doesn't make a difference to me."

"Fine." She turned off the TV and tossed the remote onto the coffee table. "If you're going to act like that, I'll come."

Great. That meant she'd sit there being cranky and somehow put the blame on us.

"Where should we go?" Gram asked.

I answered before my mom could. "I was thinking Emilio's."

Gram smiled at me, bouncing the palms of her hands together almost as if she were clapping, but without any sound. "I haven't been there in ages! Just let me get my slippers and run a comb through my hair." She began the tedious process of getting up, squaring her feet underneath her and trying to rock her weight forward out of her chair.

But my mom was still sitting on the couch, frowning at me. "Why there? There are so many other restaurants. Let's go someplace new."

Gram froze, her broad hips hanging precariously off the front of her seat, her hands braced on the arms, ready to push herself up.

"We're going to Emilio's." I wasn't about to let her make an issue out of it, either. I wanted to see Vin.

"I hate it there. Frank Fierro is so rude—"

"He is not."

"He never talks to me, and when he does, he looks down his nose at me."

"You're imagining things."

"No, I'm not. You never understand, but I won't go. I won't give them our good money for their lousy food while he sits there judging me."

"The food isn't lousy. And it's not *our* money. It's *my* money." I looked at Gram. Her eyebrows were up, but I could tell she didn't disapprove of my tone.

Mom decided to change her attack. "But still, Trey. Emilio's is so old-fashioned. If we're celebrating, we may as well go someplace nice. How about that cute little sushi place over on Roosevelt?"

"That'll cost twice as much, and Gram doesn't like sushi." Plus, I'd have zero chance of cornering Vinnie.

"They have teriyaki—"

"Enough." I held my hand up as if I could ward off her bullshit. "It's really simple: Gram and I are going to Emilio's. You can stay here and pout, or you can come with us and try to have a good time. But I swear to God, Mom, if you come and spend the entire evening griping and complaining and generally making my night out miserable, I'll get up and leave you there to find your own way home."

Her eyes went wide. "So now I make you miserable?"

"No, Mom. That's not what I said."

"It's always my fault, isn't it? You make decisions without me. You never consider my feelings. But somehow, it's my fault, isn't it?"

I looked over at Gram. She shook her head in resignation and heaved herself out of her seat. "Trey and I are leaving, Mindy," she said.

"What about me?"

Gram didn't even glance at her as she shuffled across the room. "There are leftovers in the fridge."

I was glad when we were finally able to leave the house. For the first three blocks, neither Gram nor I said anything, both of us trying to fight our way out of the dark cloud Mom had thrown over the outing. It helped that the weather was gorgeous.

"We should have gone to the park and had a picnic," Gram said at last. "A shame to waste this weather."

I hoped she wasn't still thinking about Mom and her fit. "We can go later, if you want. I don't work."

Gram smiled sadly and patted my hand. "Don't worry about it." She drew a deep breath and stood up straighter. "I don't know about you, but I can't wait to get some of Marco's garlic bread. It's been years."

Had it really been that long since Gram had been to the restaurant? I realized how seldom we went out, and when we did, we usually got takeout from Subway. I thought about how often I hit the restaurant on my way to or from school or work and felt guilty. "You should have said. We could have done this sooner."

Gram shrugged. "We're doing it now." Her eyes danced. "I used to practically live there. We all did, back in the day. I used to sit at the counter in as short a skirt as my mother would let me out of the house in, trying to catch one of the boys' eyes."

I laughed. "Gram! I had no idea."

"That I was such a tart? Oh yes. Trying to catch a Fierro was tricky business. You had to be pretty but coy. They do tend to be overly protective."

Didn't Trey know it. "So did you ever succeed?"

"I married your grandfather, so no. But I thought for awhile I had the oldest one's eye."

"Frank? You were sweet on *Frank*? He's like a thousand years old."

"He graduated a year ahead of me," Gram said, her voice heavy with warning.

"He did? God, he doesn't look it."

Gram's expression changed to pity. "Yes, poor thing. Christina died so young, and he had to raise all three of the children on his own. We all tried to do what we could to help out, but he was so proud, and he made it hard."

It was odd, thinking of all that old history, realizing some of it still played out in a way today. I glanced down at Gram's sensible trousers. "Do you want to go back and change? Your pink dress looks pretty good, and it lands above your knee."

As I'd meant it to, this made her laugh and ruffle my hair. We were still grinning as we entered the restaurant, but when I caught sight of who was sitting at the bar, my heart leapt up in a very different kind of joy.

Vinnie was here.

"Sophia!" Frank Fierro came out from behind the bar and opened his arms to Gram, pulling her into an embrace. "I thought maybe you'd forgotten all about us, you've been away so long."

Gram swatted his arm playfully. She smiled at him, settling in for a chat. "Don't be silly. Now tell me all about your grandbabies. I hear you have a new one?"

I slipped around them and made my way to the bar, trying not to smile too brightly lest I scare him away. "Hey, Vin. How's it going?"

He glanced up, and the boredom in his eyes turned to something like horror—the kind of horror usually reserved for bad slasher movies. I may as well have been wearing a fucking hockey mask and wielding a giant machete. I would have laughed, if it hadn't hurt so much. It confirmed what I'd already suspected: he didn't want to see me.

"Hey," he said. His cheeks were quickly flushing an alarming shade of red.

"How've you been?" I asked.

"Fine."

An awkward silence while I waited for him to start acting like a normal human being, but that was obviously more than he could handle at the moment.

"I'm good too," I said. "Thanks for asking."

His jaw clenched, and I thought maybe I'd pissed him off, but his good Catholic upbringing beat out whatever he really wanted to say. "Look," he began, and I knew he was about to offer me a halfhearted apology, so I cut him off.

"It's fine." I smiled at him in an attempt to trick him into relaxing half a degree. "I just wanted to tell you I had a good time the other night."

Clearly, not the way to get him to relax. He looked downright alarmed. He glanced around nervously, obviously worried somebody would hear, but there wasn't anybody else in the restaurant.

"The polite thing to say is, 'I had a great time too, Trey.'"

"I—"

"I wondered if you might want to do it again?"

It took him a second to answer, but then he said, "I don't think so."

It was about what I'd expected. I had no intention of letting him off the hook so easily.

"Why not?" I asked.

"Because—"

"Don't you like me?"

His blush had been fading, but now he was bright red again. He couldn't look at me. "I, umm... I don't..."

"You had fun the other night too, right? I mean, it *felt* like you were having fun."

"Oh, Christ," he swore. He tilted his head back, rocking on his heels, covering his eyes with one hand.

He wasn't denying it, though. That was the thing. He was flustered and uncomfortable and embarrassed, but only because I was right. It made my heart race. It made the butterflies in my stomach go into overdrive. It also gave me courage.

"Go out with me tonight."

"I can't."

"You *can*. We can go to dinner, or a movie. Or we could go back to that same club, or a new club. We could play Putt-Putt, for all I care. What do you say?"

"Listen," he said, meeting my eyes at last, "what happened the other night was—"

"Fun?"

"No—"

"Great?"

"No—"

"Hot as hell?"

"*No!*"

"But it was."

He took a deep breath and looked me in the eye. "It was an accident."

"An *accident?*"

"Right."

I knew what he was trying to say, and yet it annoyed me to

no end. I waited for him to either explain, or to realize how stupid he sounded, but he just stood there, like he actually thought I'd mistake his explanation for some kind of logical answer. "Let me make sure I have this right," I said at last. "You *accidentally* wandered down to Boystown, and *accidentally* went into a club. And then you *accidentally* followed me to another gay bar where we *accidentally* found ourselves groin to groin on the dance floor and *accidentally* had the fucking hottest, sexiest dance since Patrick Swayze taught that chick at summer camp to dirty dance. Like, *that kind* of accident?"

I could tell right away I'd let my sarcasm go too far. I'd been trying to loosen him up, but what I'd done instead was piss him off. He stood up straight. He put his shoulders back, and the look he gave me almost made me change my mind about wanting to see him again. He looked at me like...

Like he wanted to call me a fag and throw me out of his life.

"You've got the wrong guy. I don't do this. I don't date guys."

Despite the absurdity of it all, I didn't want to argue. If he was on the defensive, we'd never get anywhere. I wanted to appease him, and that meant I had to stop giving him a hard time and start being sincere.

I held my hands up in surrender. "I get it, Vin. I really do. It's okay. I didn't mean a date. Last time wasn't a date either, remember?" I smiled when I said that. He didn't smile back, but the anger was fading from his eyes.

"Okay." He nodded gruffly, almost in thanks, and he started to turn away.

I spoke quickly before he could. "Maybe we could have a *not-date* like that again. That's all."

He didn't seem to know how seriously to take me, but at least he'd stopped being pissed.

I stepped closer, and although he looked a bit alarmed, he let me. He stood perfectly still. "You don't date guys?" I said.

"That's fine. I don't date guys either."

His eyebrow went up at that. He almost smiled. "So," he said, "you're not gay either?"

His tone was teasing. Slightly sarcastic. Somehow, he was making fun of himself more than of me, and it made me smile. "I hate to break it to you, but I'm queer as a three-dollar bill." I was glad when he actually laughed.

I took another step toward him. Then a second. We were only a few inches from each other. His cheeks started to turn red again, but he didn't back away.

"The thing is, Vinnie, for most guys I meet, 'date' means 'sex'. Nobody ever has one without the other. But I..." I looked down at the floor, trying to figure out how to finish my sentence. *I don't have sex? I'm still a virgin? I'm not that easy?*

"You don't *date*," he said pointedly.

I thought maybe he was teasing, but when I glanced up, I was surprised at what I saw. Yes, he was amused, but there was something else in his eyes too. Maybe not respect. Not quite. But I thought maybe he understood. That hint of fear I'd been seeing since I'd walked in the door was gone.

"Right." I was relieved he understood. "I don't date."

He smiled at me, finally. That goddamn cute, quirky, smartass smile like I'd seen the other night, and I knew I was on the right track.

"So," I said, "since *you* don't date, and *I* don't date, how about if we *not* date together?"

He crossed his arms over his chest, looking thoughtful.

"Tonight?" he asked.

My heart just about jumped out of my chest. It took a conscious effort to not squeal and start bouncing like a teenage girl. "I'd love to."

Chapter Eight

Even though it wasn't actually a date, Vince was determined to get everything right.

He went to the address Kyle had given him with the tickets. As it turned out, Kyle was in, and the man welcomed him with a smile and urged him to have a seat in his office.

"I can't stay long," Vince warned. "I just wondered if you had seats available for a show tonight, unless it's too short of notice."

"Oh yes! Absolutely. Some nice ones off center left." He smiled as he scribbled something on a piece of paper. "Just take this to the box office and they'll give you what you need. Have you seen *Icarus* before, or will this be your first time?"

Vince hadn't even known what the play was. He realized he should have asked about that. "Uh, no. Is it—?" He cut himself off from saying "good" at the last second. "Does it have a happy ending?"

Kyle looked thoughtful. "Difficult question. I don't know that I'd call it a tragedy, but there aren't rainbows and puppies at the end, either. A good discussion piece for after, is how I'd describe it." He gave Vince a sly look. "Good date piece, in other words."

There was absolutely no reason to blush, which was why it annoyed Vince that he did. "Well, I don't know that it's a date."

"Ah, one of those," Kyle said wryly. "I remember the days." He passed the paper over. "Best of luck to you. I hope the show helps push you over the mark into a romantic kiss on the doorstep after, at the very least."

Vince nodded and tried to murmur his thanks, but it probably sounded like little more than a grunt to Kyle. Hurrying out of the office, he hit the box office, got the tickets and went back home to look for dinner reservations.

His choices around Theater Wit, where the production was held, were an American restaurant, an Italian place and Flat Top, a make-your-own-stir-fry place. Italian was obviously out unless he wanted to face a herd of outraged family, but he still couldn't decide between the other two. The American place sounded too boring, but what if Trey didn't want stir-fry? What if it only sounded okay and actually wasn't?

Well, it wouldn't matter then, would it, because this isn't a date.

In the end he decided to forget the whole thing and searched Urbanspoon for something entirely different. He settled on Tango Sur, an Argentine BYOB steakhouse. He knew Trey ate meat, because he'd seen him do it.

Breathing a little easier after having made a reservation, Vince got on with the rest of his preparations.

The only other hiccups came when he tried to get dressed and when he fumbled over transportation. There wasn't much to do about his clothes; he only had three suits, and he looked like a frumpy old man in all of them. He didn't think anything else he had would be dressy enough. Though maybe he shouldn't dress up too much. What if he wore a suit and Trey was in jeans?

As for the other, he'd told Trey he'd pick him up at six—but in what? A cab? With an EL ticket? Usually on dates he got his car out of storage and drove, but would that be too date-like?

Why the hell was this so *hard*? It was supposed to be women who were difficult. Who knew not-dating a man would be even worse?

In the end he became paralyzed by indecision on both

counts and called Rachel. Which meant he had to confess about Trey before he explained what help he needed.

It was both more difficult and easier than he'd thought.

"So Trey Giles is gay? I always wondered. Funny, he's never brought a date by the restaurant. Because you know we'd have heard about it. Oh—you don't think he thinks we're all homophobic, do you?"

"I don't know. I don't think he dates much. Which is why I want to get this right. Even though it isn't actually a date," he added quickly.

"You *should* date him. Trey is a sweetheart. Just don't be a dick to him."

"Rachel," Vince said in warning.

"Yes, yes. I'll be right over."

Vince glanced at his watch. "Rach, it's almost five now."

"Like I said, I'll be right over."

She hung up, and Vince spent a frantic twenty minutes driving himself crazy. When the door opened and Rachel swept in, he almost pounced on her before she could even get her key out of the lock.

"*Relax,*" she told him, taking his shoulders and turning him around to aim him at his bedroom. "Show me what we're working with."

Rachel ended up putting him in a pair of suit pants but with a dark plum-colored shirt with iridescent silver pinstripes she dug out of the back of his closet. He tried to shoot it down, because it had always felt too flashy to him, but Rachel insisted.

"You're gay now, big brother. You can be a little flashy."

"I am *not gay.*"

"Right. You're just making yourself a nervous wreck over a night out with a man. Completely different story."

Vince ran a hand over his face. "Shit. Maybe this is a

mistake."

Rachel pushed his hand away and cupped his chin. "Stop. Stop this right now. You're either going on this date or you aren't. Stop worrying about your machismo cred. Fierro boys, gay or straight, don't stand up dates. Or not-dates. You told Trey you'd be there at six; you're going to be there at six." She looked him up and down and smiled appreciatively. "And you'll probably make him melt into a puddle, which is as it should be."

Vince turned to the mirror, braced for the worst, but to his surprise he found that he actually looked pretty damn good. Except...he fussed with his collar. "I need a necklace or something, though, don't you think?" He rooted around on his dresser for a gold chain.

Rachel laughed. "Yes, Italian boy. Add a single red rose and you'll probably get laid for sure."

"No." Vince put the chain he'd found back down, unsure now. "That's the deal. Trey doesn't do that."

"What, get laid?" When Vince simply stared at her, Rachel's eyes widened, and then they softened. "Oh, Vinnie." She kissed him on the cheek. "You're such a good boy, you know that? I hope it does work out with Trey. I hope this evens everything out for you, that it really is your magic bullet. I'd love to see you happy." She patted his shoulder. "Now put on your gold chain. Even if it does scream Hot Italian Sex Machine, there's no harm in making Trey desperate."

"You're vicious," Vince said, watching his reflection in the mirror as he reached around to fasten the chain.

"Yes." Rachel took the clasp from his hands, finished it, then dusted him off. "Go get on the EL, walk up to his door and ask him if he wants a cab or a train. Traffic in the Loop will be hell at this hour, so you might as well not even try to drive both ways."

That was a good plan. Vince took a deep breath, let it out and squared his shoulders.

"Okay?" Rachel asked.

"Okay," Vince agreed.

Chapter Nine

I had all day to think about the date that wasn't a date. As the afternoon wore on I began to realize one thing: I had no idea what to expect.

Where would we go? Why hadn't I thought to ask? Where would macho, Italian, "I'm not gay" Vin take a boy like me? One thing I was absolutely certain of: he would go to great lengths to keep things casual. He'd want to make sure it felt like something other than a date. I figured I was looking at some kind of male bonding, boys' night out. It was possible we'd end up bowling and drinking Bud out of a can.

In the end, I narrowed it down to the three most likely scenarios: a movie—probably one with explosions and plenty of bosom. A restaurant—probably a sports bar. Or, best-case scenario, back to the jazz club, where we could dance—and I'd be lying if I said that option didn't make my heart skip a beat and my blood head for places south of my brain. In truth, I didn't care where we went, so long as I had a chance to flirt with him a bit.

I had to go into campus to do a little research at the library that afternoon, and I was childishly impatient on the way home. The EL seemed to be moving half its normal speed. I fidgeted in my seat and checked my watch repeatedly, just to assure myself that I did indeed still have plenty of time. I practically skipped up the front steps to my door.

I walked into my own private version of hell.

If there's one certainty about living with an alcoholic, it's that nothing is ever certain. Nothing, that is, except the next relapse.

My mom had been sober for three months this time. Three months where we all smiled and laughed and acted like a happy family. Three months where we all pretended like we believed it might last this time. I knew as soon as I walked in the front door that her clean streak was over.

There are a lot of stereotypes about alcoholism, most of which look like some kind of movie of the week: screaming, yelling, blackouts. In my early teens, I'd seen the movie *The Burning Bed*. I'd been haunted by the character of Paul and the cruel, sadistic, almost sexual heat in his eyes as he stared at his wife and calmly told his kids to go to bed so that he could do unspeakable things to her. I'd thought over and over about how much he deserved what he got. Yet at no point did I connect his illness with my mother's disease.

Disease.

I fucking hated that word.

The beast that ruled our house wasn't full of rage or violence. There were no screaming fits or visits from the police. My mother's alcoholism was the clichéd elephant in the living room. The weight around our necks that had settled in after my father had died, the silent beast we tiptoed around and pretended not to see.

The house was eerily still, yet not silent. My mother sat alone on the couch, watching Home Shopping Network with blurry and unfocused eyes. The cheery chatter of the saleslady on the television seemed false and obnoxious.

I found my grandmother in the kitchen unloading the dishwasher. Her shoulders were permanently stooped, her fingers crooked from the arthritis. She had weak knees that were aggravated by the extra weight around her hips. She had to move with exaggerated slowness, putting away one dish at a time, shuffling from one side of the kitchen to the other in her muumuu and slippers.

"Gram, you don't have to do that," I told her. "You know I'll take care of it."

She waved her hand at me dismissively. "It does me good to move around."

This is one of the games we play, as we dance around this "disease". The truth was, my grandma couldn't stand to sit in the living room with my mother, watching her sway, listening to her slurred words. My mother would stare resolutely ahead, refusing to acknowledge that she'd done anything wrong. It was easier for my grandmother to occupy herself with chores than to face what her daughter-in-law had become.

"I forgot to thaw the hamburger for dinner," she told me. "How about some nice fish sticks?"

"It's okay, Gram. I won't be here. I have a..." Not a date. "I have plans."

"Oh?" She turned to me with a twinkle in her eye. "What lucky boy has finally talked you into going out?"

While my mother did her best to pretend my homosexuality didn't exist, my grandmother seemed to find a reckless kind of joy in it. She teased me all the time about finding a nice boy. I felt myself blush under her curious scrutiny. "It's Vin," I said. "Vin Fierro."

Her eyes widened in surprise. "Little Vinnie?" She shook her head. "I never would have guessed."

"I don't think he's really out, Gram, so don't do anything to embarrass him, okay?"

"Okay. Okay." She turned back to the dishwasher with a sigh. "I guess you saw."

Another step in the dance, acknowledging without saying the words. "I did."

"Are you meeting Vincent out somewhere?" Another step, moving on to the next subject before we could say anything that might actually matter.

"He's picking me up at six."

She glanced at the clock and *tsk*ed her tongue. "You better start getting ready. You don't want to keep him waiting."

Translation: You don't want to have to let him in the house.

"You're right."

A short, cool shower, and I didn't even let myself jerk off. I wanted to savor the lingering sense of arousal that Vin had kindled in me. I dressed quickly. I assumed our "not date" would be casual, so I didn't dress up. I chose clothes I might have worn to the club if I'd actually been cruising—tight jeans with some strategically placed holes and a silky soft V-neck shirt that hugged my skin. Not like I had huge muscles to show off, but a slim waist and a perfectly flat stomach could be just as appealing to the right man. I hoped Vin was one of them. My one true vanity was my hair, which had to be exactly the right kind of messy. I fussed with that until the doorbell rang at four minutes to six. He was nothing if not punctual.

I rushed into the living room, ready to head off my mother in case she'd thought to answer the door, but she was still sitting on the couch, swaying in her seat, staring blankly ahead. She clutched something in her hand, something small that I couldn't quite make out, something smaller than a fifth. I assumed it was a travel-sized bottle she'd picked up from the corner store.

I turned away, trying to put her out of my mind.

"Bye, Gram!" I called out. "Don't wait up." With any luck, I'd be home late.

I opened the door and found Vin looking like some kind of uber-Italian Rico Suave. Jesus Christ, he looked like fucking sex on a stick. Not only that, but he looked *nice*. Not casual nice. *Date* nice. I half-expected him to offer me a corsage. Mister "this isn't a date" Vin Fierro was pressed and ironed, his hair combed, a gold chain glinting at his open collar. For all of his words of denial, this apparently *was* a date.

A date for which I was embarrassingly underdressed.

He raised his eyebrow at me in that smartass way of his. "You ready?"

Fuck. Now what? On a good day, I would have invited him in while I ran to my room and changed, but that would mean having him see my mother. He'd feel compelled to make small talk with her. She would blink blurrily at him. When she spoke, her words would come out jumbled and incomprehensible. She would be, in a word, unbearable.

"Umm..." I looked down at my clothes, trying to decide how rude it would be to ask him to wait on the porch while I changed. But then I looked up at him again.

He was staring at me. Not at my face, but in the general vicinity of my waist. A slow blush was creeping up his cheeks.

Maybe I wouldn't change my clothes after all.

"Give me one second," I told him.

I ignored the confusion on his face as I closed the door, leaving him standing on the porch. I ran to my room and pulled open my closet. A silk scarf my Gram had bought me went around my neck. My one sport coat went over it all. Leather shoes replaced my Converse.

A glance in the mirror and I decided it would have to do. Yes, Vin looked like the ultimate personification of Italian machismo, and I looked like a poster boy for the ACLU. What did it matter?

After all, this wasn't a date.

Chapter Ten

Vince stared at the closed door to Trey's brownstone, battling confusion and beating back panic while the tips of his ears heated. The latter gave him something else to focus on, and he touched them self-consciously, first the left and the right, worrying they would be so red that Trey would notice. He peered into the glass beside the door, seeking out his reflection to check the state of his ears for himself.

He saw, merged with his monochromatic reflection, a pale, haggard female face surrounded by thin and scraggly blonde-gray hair peering back at him. Frowning, Vince crouched down and squinted, wondering who in the hell it was. Before he could identify her, he heard Trey's muffled voice call out "Mom!" and then "Gram?" from inside the house. The face at the window turned away before disappearing altogether. Scuffling sounds merged with urgent, hushed voices behind the door, wrapping around a sharp, slurred voice objecting in words Vince couldn't quite make out. Silence fell.

The door opened and Trey all but leapt out of it, closing it so quickly behind him Vince wouldn't have been surprised to hear the thud of some wild animal's paws on the back of the door.

"Everything okay?" Vince asked.

"Yes." The word shot out of Trey so hard it nearly left an imprint in Vince's chest. Vince opened his mouth to press, because very clearly everything wasn't okay, but at that same moment his brain registered the subtle changes in Trey's outfit and reminded him how incredibly alluring the young man's waistline was, even half-hidden by a jacket.

A sharp, slurred complaint from inside jolted Vince out of his lust-filled stupor. It also prompted Trey to grab Vince's arm and pull him down the stairs with a tight-voiced, "Let's get going."

Vince let himself be dragged down to the sidewalk, and when Trey didn't let go, he increased his pace to stalk alongside. His concern did battle with a sense of acute pleasure at Trey's hand on his arm. The slim, sure grip anchored him and drew him like a tractor beam. Fleeting analysis of men versus women's touch gave way to simple pleasure, leaving him bereft when Trey stopped at the corner to cross and allowed him to realize what he was doing.

"Sorry." Trey drew back, flinching. The hand which had held Vince's arm shot into Trey's hair and tightened into a fist as Trey's bright, handsome face closed off.

The roller coaster Vince had been riding all day didn't exactly pull into the station, but it did come to a strange out-of-body sort of pause. Ever since he'd agreed to a not-date, in fact, he'd existed in at least a low-grade panic. But as he stood with Trey on the corner of his block, he realized that since the moment Trey had opened the door, there had been no panic, not until he'd closed the door and gone away again. Now the panic was gone entirely, and in its place he found a mild confusion over what exactly had happened back there at the door and a rapidly deepening happiness at simply being with Trey. Being out on a date with Trey, because no matter what they called it out loud, Vince was willing to admit to himself that it *was* a date.

What his date needed right now was to relax.

Glancing at his watch, Vince nodded at a half-lit sign up the street. "We have plenty of time before the show. What do you say we put in a round of darts and drinks first?" If anything, Trey's face closed off even more. Vince scanned farther up the street, mentally mapping the surrounding neighborhood as well. "Or how about Orecchio's?"

Trey's entire body seemed to exhale as he turned to grin at Vince, eyes sparkling. "I haven't been there since I was ten."

"Well past time to go back." Vince put a hand on Trey's lower back and steered him east.

Orecchio's was a fixture for any kid who had grown up in the neighborhood: a pizza parlor and game room serving as a mom-and-pop version of the nationwide chains. Orecchio's hosted fewer games and better pizza and didn't require driving to DePaul or Gage Park, making it a favorite of parents and indulgent uncles, Vince included.

Once inside, however, Vince worried at the wisdom of his choice. Tonight, as ever, shrieking children tore up the tile floor between the game room and the main floor of the restaurant where parents dolled out fives and twenties to buy themselves another half hour of fragile peace. Would only-child Trey see this as a circus, despite his initial nostalgia?

Glancing at Trey, Vince relaxed to see his date smiling, wistful remembrances of childhood past still in place. Inspired by the telltale *clunk-roll-clunk* rumbling beneath the chaotic chorus of electronic beeps and sirens, Vince fished a ten out of his pocket and waved it in front of Trey's face. "How about I beat you at some skee-ball?"

Oh, but Vince loved it when Trey's eyes lit up like that. "Sure, I can let you win, if it'll make you feel better."

Laughing, Vince indicated the change machine with the bill. "I'll just get us some tokens, and then we'll see who beats whom."

The machines were the same exact ones from when Vince was a kid, including the temperamental one against the far wall that could be talked out of an extra ball with a few well-placed nudges. Despite securing that advantage, Vince had to work hard to keep up with Trey, and eventually he had to concede defeat as Trey steadily and soundly whipped his ass.

"I used to come here with my mom all the time," Trey confessed. "She taught me how to aim for the 100s."

Vince knew how to aim for them too, but his skill paled next to Trey's. He shook his head, grinning. "I come here every other weekend with my nieces and nephews. Even with that much practice, you're kicking my butt."

"I noticed." Trey dropped in a new token, keeping his eye on the target rings. "Should we order a pizza? As the loser, you buy, but I've got the next round of tokens." When Vince glanced at his watch, Trey paused, second ball clutched in his fist. "Oh—sorry. Am I messing up your plans? We can just go."

Vince placed a hand over his left pants pocket. "Well, I'd meant to take us to a steakhouse, but that's no big deal. We can eat here instead. The thing is, I have these tickets for a play at eight. I'd say let's ditch it, but they were kind of a favor, and…"

Vince could feel his ears heating again. He ducked his head to avoid having to meet Trey's eyes, but Trey didn't let him escape so easily. The boy stepped closer, stooping a bit to get into Vinnie's line of sight, forcing Vinnie to look at him.

"You're taking me to a play?"

"Up in Lakeside. It's called *Icarus*. It's supposed to be good. But if you really don't want to go, I'll just apologize tomorrow. No worries."

Trey said nothing, but he reached out and touched Vinnie's sleeve. Vince combed the blank face in front of him over and over, desperately searching for a clue as to whether or not he was in trouble.

"You dressed up. You were taking me to a steakhouse and now you tell me there's a play which you called in a favor to get tickets to." The corner of Trey's mouth tipped up. "If this is what you do for a not-date, I can't help but wonder what you do for the real deal."

Vince shrugged, but he was smiling too. "The usual. Limo

with champagne up Lake Shore Drive and candlelight picnic in front of Buckingham Fountain."

"That must get cold in the winter."

"Oh, winter." Vince's mind sped ahead of his tongue. "Winter is different, of course. Then it's a romantic cabin in Wisconsin."

Trey rolled his eyes, but he was still grinning. "And ice skating, I suppose."

"Ice fishing," Vince corrected. When Trey laughed, Vince feigned offense. "Hey, I wouldn't want to be a cliché."

Trey punched him playfully in the arm, but instead of pulling away his fingers lingered as he leaned closer. "Tell you what. Let's get a pizza, hustle up to the play, and to close off our not-date you can take me dancing again."

An electric thrill rushed through Vince's bloodstream, settling into a low-grade hum at his groin. "Dancing?" he repeated, his mind recalling the sensations of holding Trey close.

"Dancing. At the jazz club." Trey ran a finger down Vince's forearm. "What do you say?"

Hell yes, Vince's dick shouted. His mouth said, "What do you want on your pizza? To get your strength up for dancing."

Trey's smile could have lit up half of Chicago. "Everything."

Chapter Eleven

Vince didn't understand the play exactly, but it didn't matter, because he was almost positive that Trey had a great time. Vince had a good time too, but it was because he was there with Trey.

Kyle had given him the old eyebrow when Vince came in with a guy, and for a minute he'd panicked. For what he wasn't sure, and as he'd realized that, he forced himself to relax. He greeted Kyle and introduced Trey. Kyle gave them some complimentary drink tickets and a wink, and that was that.

Nothing to panic about.

After the show they went to the bar Trey had taken them to that first night when Vince had gone out. They didn't hold hands on the way, which would have been weird, but they did walk closely together on the sidewalk, which was nice.

"Why do I hardly ever see you at the restaurant anymore?" Trey asked. "Too much family?"

Vince shook his head. "No such thing. I just..." He paused, trying to think of how to phrase it. "Well, this sounds nuts, but sometimes being in the middle of all that family can be very lonely."

Trey frowned. "I never thought about it. There's just me and Gram and my mom. I can't even imagine what it must be like to have cousins and stuff."

"I have plenty of those. Let me know when you want to borrow them."

They walked in silence for awhile. A group of young guys

laughing and looking inebriated took up too much of the sidewalk, and even after Vince moved far to the left, practically hugging the side of a building, they were set to run Trey right over. Without thinking, Vince put his arm around Trey and shifted their positions, huddling around him and putting his back to the drunks. As they buffeted Vince's back, he glanced down at Trey, who was gazing up at him, eyes sparkling.

Vince smiled.

Trey smiled back, the light in his eyes spreading to the rest of his face.

When the drunks were past, Vince went back to the center of the sidewalk, but he found his arm lingered against Trey's back, and he left it there as long as he could until it seemed awkward. As he let it fall, though, Trey took hold of his biceps.

It felt good.

Being with Trey felt good. Going out with him—on a date, yeah. So what? So he was dating a guy. So he was...gay, or whatever. What the fuck did it matter? He was having a good time. He was happy. He'd played skee-ball and watched a play and now was going to go dancing. They'd laughed and ate pizza and talked and talked, more than Vince thought he had on a date, ever.

There was nothing here to freak out over, just like Rachel said. And he wanted to do this again. The thought made his insides jump all over the place, like a skee-ball was rattling around inside him hitting nothing but 100s.

The jazz bar was a lot busier than it had been the other night they'd come, but it was still ten times more pleasant than that awful gay bar where he'd met up with Trey the last time. A live band played "In a Sentimental Mood" almost as good as Ellington and Coltrane. The dance floor was full, as was the bar, and all the tables. He caught a glance of himself in the mirror and saw that Rach was right, he looked damn fine. Trey too, and the two of them looked good together.

Vince grinned. All he needed was a scotch and a cigar and the moment would be damn near perfect.

He nodded to the bar. "Want anything to drink?"

"Water, please."

"Sure thing." Vince pulled out his wallet and elbowed into a free space to order. He got a bottle of water for Trey and a scotch neat for himself.

Trey took the water and smiled, but Vince couldn't help but notice his date's gaze drift down to his scotch, and that his expression went a little flat at the sight of the drink. If he hadn't indulged in a single malt call, he might have put it aside and forgotten about it.

Instead he sipped even more casually than normal and kept watching Trey for clues as to why his ordering a scotch was such a bad thing. They stood there for a few minutes, until the song ended. When a new one started, Vince eased back happily against the wall behind him.

"Somebody in this band likes Coltrane." He took a sip of his scotch and basked in the sultry saxophone. "I like this band."

"Do you listen to a lot of jazz?"

"Oh yeah. But Coltrane is my favorite. Nobody has been able to make a sax sing like he could. These guys don't do too badly."

Trey leaned against the wall too, but he sagged a bit against Vince's side. "It's so...I don't know. Not soft, but relaxing. Easy. I feel like I could float away."

"That's the idea. Jazz seduces you." Seeing that Trey had drained his water bottle, Vince took one more sip of scotch, leaned over to put the unfinished glass on the bar and held out his hand. "Ready to dance?"

Beaming, Trey took his hand.

They found a bit of open floor space up front by the band. Vince herded them off to the side, in part because he was still a little self-conscious about dancing with a man, in part because it was dark there, and he liked the idea of dancing in the dark with Trey.

Still, when Trey settled into his arms, fitting their bodies close together, Vince watched the other couples to see who was watching him. A few were, though most didn't seem to care, too wrapped up in each other. Maybe some of those who noticed looked like they didn't care for two guys dancing. Maybe he read into it.

They weren't the only same-sex couple on the floor, either. Two other male couples and a female pair were scattered amongst the heterosexuals. Realizing he'd just lumped himself in with the not-heterosexual crowd, the skee-ball went berserk inside Vince again, this time finding every gutter.

He shut his eyes and tried to shut off his stupid head, tried instead to focus on Trey.

It was a good distraction. God, but Trey just *fit* in his arms. A lot of women had, yeah, but not like this. It felt completely different to hold a man. Trey's body was harder, more filled out, and in more than that hard ridge pressing against the front of Vince's trousers. He smelled different too. Like a man. And it was so...right.

The band was playing Sinatra now, a smooth-voiced tenor singing "Like Someone in Love". Vince pulled Trey closer, fitting their bodies so tight together they were nearly fused. He didn't hide his erection, and when Trey shifted against him, subtly increasing the friction in time to the beat, Vince didn't let it do anything but fuel the pleasure of the moment.

Trey nuzzled Vince's neck, his nose, then his lips brushing Vince's collar, his skin. "Vinnie?"

"Mmm?" Vince nuzzled back.

Trey's lips moved along Vince's jaw, tickled his ear. "This is a date."

Vince grinned and rubbed the scruff of his cheek alongside Trey's. "Yeah."

Those tickling lips brushed his lobe, and a tongue darted out, making Vince shiver. "I want another one."

The tongue had made Vince shiver, but those words shimmied right down to the bottom of his belly. "Sure."

Slim hands gripped his hips, fingers curling into his backside. "I want a kiss."

The heat slid lower, setting all of Vince into a slow, steady burn. He didn't say anything, just pulled his head back far enough to meet Trey's gaze, angle his head and close in on his mouth.

It started almost sweet, but they were both hard, both kneading hands into each other, and fuck if Trey didn't taste more exotic than anything in the world. He worried for a second that Trey would dislike the scotch on his breath, but then Trey pushed him deeper into the shadows, into an alcove behind the speaker, and Vince didn't worry about anything at all.

There was something incredibly freeing about being this turned on and being somewhat secluded. They were hidden but at the same time couldn't go too far because they were still, technically, on a dance floor in a respectable establishment. Much as he wanted to undo Trey's pants and take his cock in hand, as ready as he suddenly was for that kind of thing, he couldn't, and it was a little bit of a relief.

Instead he ground against Trey's pelvis like he was trying to screw him to the wall, and the soft, gasping noises Trey made only inspired Vince to dig his fingers deeper into Trey's backside. The kiss was deep and crazy, mouths mating, tongues tangling, Trey's hands pulling Vince in closer and closer until they almost couldn't breathe. Vince's nipples pebbled beneath his shirt, so stiff they jutted like rocks, super-sensitized points that made him moan against Trey's lips.

Eventually the delicious tease turned over though, and common sense warned Vince he needed to slow the fuck down or he was going to come all over the inside of his pants. Trey seemed to be in a similar place, because when Vince pulled back, easing out of the kiss slowly, Trey didn't draw him back, just held on tight, breathing hard.

When he was able, Vince said, "Will that do?"

Trey smiled like the sun itself, and even in the dark Vince could see the sparkle in those eyes. "Yeah."

They stayed at the jazz club until a little past midnight. They danced, but they caught a table too and had a couple of sodas while Vince nudged Trey into telling him about school, idle stuff like that. Trey gave him an update on the group project that was driving him crazy, the one that had started at Emilio's with the blond idiot. Trey asked about Vince's family, about what was going on at the restaurant, where his parents were planning to vacation that summer.

Vince noticed they were staying carefully away from discussing Trey's family. He wondered about that, but he didn't ask.

When they finally headed out, he ignored Trey's protests that he could go home on his own since it was completely out of Vince's way, and he rode the EL back down to Trey's house. They held hands on the train and on the walk back from the station, even though they were in full view of people who might recognize them both. Vince's dick was already humming, thinking about what had to be a kiss on the stoop, hoping that maybe they could sit on the couch and make out a little bit more, that maybe he could grab hold of Trey's cock after all. The idea wasn't even alarming anymore, just exciting.

Except as they rounded the corner to Trey's street, Trey became markedly tense, no longer sinking happily against Vince but training his gaze hard on the windows to his house. When he spoke there was a strange edge to his voice. Not anger so much as...reservation.

"My mom is still up. I would invite you in, but..." He trailed off, suddenly awkward and uncomfortable looking.

Vince's dick sang a sad, sad song. No necking on the couch, then. "That's okay. I should be heading back anyway. Work tomorrow, bright and early." He stopped them at the foot of the stairs, turned Trey so that they faced each other and looked him right in the eye. "I had a great time tonight. I hope you did too."

The smile came back to Trey's face, not as much as Vince would have liked, but it was enough. "I did. It was great." He looked like he was trying to rally himself and nudged Vince's shoe playfully with the tip of his. "So. Do I get the fountain next time, since you admit it was a date?"

Next time. Vince's face was going to split from all this grinning. "Might be a bit cold, since the weather took a turn again."

"I don't know that I'm ready for a cabin getaway yet."

"How about deep-dish pizza and the aquarium?"

Trey's eyes were dancing once more. "Saturday?"

God, Vince wished. "I have a family thing that night." He thought about inviting Trey along, but he wasn't sure he was *that* ready, not yet. "Sunday afternoon?"

"Sunday it is. How about three? I'll come to your place this time."

Vince touched Trey's cheek. "Sounds good to me."

The kiss good night wasn't as fiery as the one in the corner of the bar, but Vince almost liked it better. It was sweet and slow, more romantic than a Coltrane ballad. It wasn't a kiss of lust or wanting, not entirely. It was a courting kiss, the kind you got when you were in high school and first dating. Except Vince wasn't fifteen, and he wasn't as hormone-crazed or as hurried as he'd been then.

Trey wanted courting. Vince found, the more he thought about it, that he did too.

He watched Trey disappear into his house, watched the lights turn on inside before he turned back toward the station.

He let the evening swim through his mind on replay as he headed back home, as he undressed for bed, and as he lay awake listening to the traffic on the streets below.

No more panic. No more freaking out. He was dating Trey. He was...not entirely straight.

I'm having a good time, he tried instead, when he felt his jaw start to tense up. *I like him. He likes me. I'm happy. And we're taking our time.*

And we're going out again on Sunday.

Vince smiled, only a little nervously, into the dark.

Chapter Twelve

It was tough to face reality after my date with Vinnie. And yes, it *had* been a date.

I felt like I was flying. More than flying. It was like some crazy vibration, some wild beat within my body that kept me smiling, kept me dancing, kept my feet from ever touching the ground. I wanted to stand on my front porch with him all night, just to feel his fingertips on my cheek one more time.

Walking through my door was a rude and sudden crash landing back to earth.

"Home already?" my mom asked from the couch. "Figured you'd stay at your boyfriend's house."

"How often has that actually happened, Mom? Have I ever *not* come home?"

She shrugged, as if it were inconsequential. Her gaze never strayed from the TV.

I tossed my keys on the table. I stared at her, where she sat swaying on the couch. It seems strange to say that an alcoholic can't hold her liquor, but my mother couldn't. She became confused and clumsy. Her words came out thick and slurred and slow. Usually I could tell how drunk she was by looking at her eyes. The further down the well she was, the less able she was to keep them open. Her eyelids would droop, and she'd teeter unsteadily in her own private darkness.

She was a mess this time, her lids heavy, her mouth hanging open.

I debated going straight to my room, rather than letting

myself be dragged down by her drinking, but the anger and the rage were so hot and fresh. I couldn't let it go. I couldn't walk away again.

"Why'd you do it this time?" I asked.

"Had a tough day."

"A tough day? Doing what? Sitting here on your ass?"

She shook her head. "You don't understand."

"You're right, Mom. I don't understand. After working so hard to get sober, why would you throw it down the drain? You know how much I hate it when you drink."

Her head bobbed lazily as she nearly toppled off the couch. "It was a fur coat."

"What are you talking about?"

"I had one once."

"I know. What does that have to do with anything?"

"It was rabbit fur. It was brown and gray. It was so soft."

"I remember."

"I lost it. Your dad and I went to Boston—"

"I know." I'd heard the story a hundred times, but she continued on as if she hadn't heard me.

"—and I guess I left it at the restaurant, but we went back. Your dad looked and looked. He even tried to offer a reward, but we never found it. He was so upset."

"Mom, *I know.*"

"I still wonder if I dropped it in the parking lot, or if somebody stole it. It was rabbit fur. It was brown and gray."

"I know! I remember it!"

"We were in Boston—"

"*Mom!*"

She gestured toward the TV, which was still on some home-shopping channel. "They showed one. It was just like the one your dad bought for me."

"And?"

She shook her head. "It was so soft. Your dad looked and looked. He even offered a reward."

This was always what she did, circling back over her words, repeating herself endlessly.

"*Why are you drinking again?*"

"It's not my fault, Trey."

"Then whose fault is it?"

"It's a disease."

"Don't give me that bullshit."

"You don't understand. You never understand." Her voice caught, and tears fell from her eyes, but any sympathy I'd ever had for her had dried up years ago.

"So you saw a goddamn fur coat on the TV and decided that was a good reason to get drunk?"

"You don't understand."

"I understand that you'll use any flimsy excuse you can find."

"It's a disease. It's not my fault. I can't help it!"

"It *is* your fault! The disease didn't decide to drink. The disease didn't go find your purse. The disease didn't walk out the door and down the street to Lucky's. The disease didn't walk to the back row where the vodka is and pick the bottle up off the shelf—"

"I didn't go to Lucky's. You never understand."

"—and walk up to the register and pay for it. The disease didn't open the bottle, Mom. The disease didn't drink it, either. You did. It *is* your fault. It's always your fault."

She closed her eyes and shook her head hard, like a dog shaking water from its fur, as if she were trying to shake her thoughts into order, trying to make sense of what I was saying. The motion caused her to fall sideways a bit. She caught herself and sat there, frozen, leaning to the side, her eyes shut tight. "It was so soft. It was brown and gray. We looked and looked..."

Swearing, I turned away from her and headed for the stairs. On the way I kicked something on the floor, a small brown bottle that went immediately under the couch. Instead of picking it up, I went up the stairs and slammed my bedroom door shut behind me, thankful that my Gram was asleep and without her hearing aid wouldn't be wakened by my temper.

I threw myself down on the bed. "Fuck, fuck, fuck!" I held my pillow over my head and forced myself to take a deep breath. And another. The anger began to fade, but behind was the tired resignation I'd grown so familiar with. It brought tears to my eyes. Not sympathy for my mother, but frustration at knowing that I was on a merry-go-round that would never, ever stop.

Up and down, round and round, the same goddamn nauseating music going on and on and on. It was enough to make me wish Vinnie had asked me to go home with him. How much better would my night have been?

I probably wouldn't still be a virgin.

I took another deep, shuddering breath. Yes, the merry-go-round went on, and I'd never escape, but at least now I had a new distraction. I thought about Vinnie—the way he'd kissed me in the club, grinding against me, and again on my porch, a sweet, lingering kiss that made me giddy—and I smiled.

I shouldn't really have agreed to the date on Sunday. I had too much schoolwork to do and too little time between jobs.

On the other hand, it would give me a perfectly good excuse to spend all of my time at home locked in my room, studying.

And on Sunday, Vinnie Fierro would kiss me.

Chapter Thirteen

Counting Vince, there were currently fifty-five living and local members of the Fierro family. Counting exes, the few who had moved out of Chicago and kids away at college, the family boasted sixty-seven members. Thirty-some of those members worked for the restaurants in some fashion, both the cafe and the one downtown, though some of the work was rather loosely associated.

Vince had six living aunts and uncles on his father's side and fourteen cousins. He had four nieces and nephews and twenty-three first cousins once removed, though every last one of them called him Uncle Vin. He had a first cousin twice removed as well: Shane Giuseppe, the much-lauded fourth generation currently working at the restaurant. The poor kid was only sixteen and had dreams of going places and doing things. Vince hoped he got to live his dreams, but he wouldn't have bet much money on that happening.

The Saturday night after his date with Trey was Uncle Marco and Aunt Eva's fortieth anniversary party, which meant it was a command performance for anyone living and able to get to the original cafe. The restaurant would remain open because it always did except for Christmas and Easter, but the basement would be filled to the gills with Fierros until the upstairs closed, and then they would very likely run the place out of booze, bread and desserts. Most of the upstairs had been reserved by friends of Marco and Eva, and most of them wouldn't get to pay for their dinner, either, especially if they came with a present.

When Vince arrived, the party was already in full swing. He'd had to mingle with many of the upstairs patrons before heading to the basement party, and once there he was mobbed by children wanting his attention. Eventually he was able to get to Marco and Eva and pay his respects. Vince's mother was seated near them, and Eva and Lisa spent a good fifteen minutes fussing over him, asking if he'd found a girl yet, trying to set him up with people they knew who knew people. They were ramping up the pressure to get him to commit to a string of dates when Frank rescued him and dragged him over to the group of men at the service bar, where Vince's own father poured him a scotch.

Dino handed Vince the glass with a nod. "How's business?"

"Good." Vince sipped the scotch. "Keeping me busy."

"We're busy here," Dino said, his voice heavy with meaning. "Could really use an accountant."

"You need to stay by family," Frank added. "Don't know what will happen to an unmarried man if he strays too far from home."

Dino clapped his hand on Vince's shoulder. His dad had already had a few glasses of scotch, Vince could tell. "Your mama wants more grandbabies, son." When Vince winced, Dino laughed. "That's right. Fina has *eight*. Louis and Gilly can't have them all. You and Rachel need to get going."

"Families need babies," Frank agreed, toasting the air with his drink.

Dino met the toast. "Men need wives."

"Otherwise they end up like your cousin Hank, Vinnie. You don't want to be like Hank, do you?"

Vinnie pasted on a smile and toasted with them, drinking faster than he should and wishing the women would harass him again.

He escaped the men at the bar and mingled around in the back, where he surveyed the crowd and ate standing from his heaping plate. There would be dancing once everyone was done eating, though food would be available until it was all gone. He nodded and smiled at Rachel, who was caught in a web of female cousins and aunts giving her the same grilling he'd gotten: get married, have kids.

Within the Fierro clan only three of them were over twenty-five and unmarried: Vince, Rachel and Hank. Hank was the only one they didn't hound anymore, but sometimes the way they spoke of him, it was like he was dead already. He was ten years older than Vin, but they'd been funny about him since Vince had come out of college. Hank rarely came to family functions; he'd moved far into the northern burbs and kept to himself. When he did show up, he never had a date, not anymore, and he always looked grim.

No, Vince didn't want to end up like Hank.

He drank some wine and pondered what it would have been like to bring Trey. Could he have, he wondered? If he'd just said he was a friend? Maybe. They'd have all asked a lot of questions, many of them including his availability to be matched up for dating single Fierros. Which would mean Trey would say he was gay, and...well.

What if Vince said Trey was his date?

He laughed at himself and drank more wine.

When the dancing started, the kids found him again, and he shucked his jacket and got all hot and sweaty twirling the girls around and teaching the boys how to behave around the girls. His sister Gilly nudged him to dance with Marcie, who blushed but smiled under Vince's teasing. He did a turn with Eva too, and his mother.

At nine thirty he collapsed beside Rachel and reached for her uneaten cake.

"I'm going to sneak out for a smoke pretty soon," she murmured. "If I thought I could go for good without a lecture from Mom, I would."

"Mmm," Vince said around her cake. He wiped his mouth with a napkin and shook his head. "You wouldn't hear the end of it for a month."

Rachel groaned. "God, Vinnie. Doesn't it drive you crazy? Because I know you got the same degree of grilling I did. I swear one of these times I'm going to show up with a drug dealer, just to make them shut up." She nudged him with her elbow. "Speaking of dates. How did yours go with Trey?"

She spoke the latter quietly, but Vince still looked around nervously before replying. "Good." He took wine. "Great, actually. It was a nice time."

"You get lucky?"

Vince glared at her. "You're not getting that kind of information."

She arched an eyebrow at him. "Do you even know how to get lucky with Trey?"

Not really, no. He had ideas, obviously. He'd admit to a little web recon, and hadn't that been an adventure unto itself. He picked up a bite of cake and held it toward her. "Here. Put this in your mouth."

She pushed it away and rose. "Come on. Let's go smoke."

They went out the back door that led up from the basement into an alley, heading down a few buildings and obscuring themselves behind a doorway. Rachel passed Vince a cigarette, and he took it and the lighter from her, setting up a flame and a protective shield via his palm for her before lighting up himself. The smoke burned his lungs and the nicotine buzzed at his brain, and within three puffs he was feeling a whole lot better.

He ashed out into the alley. "What do you think would happen if I brought Trey to a gig like this?"

"As a date, you mean?"

"Yeah."

Rachel took a long drag and blew out before replying. "I don't know. I really don't. I'd like to think they'd get over it fast because it was Trey, but—well, Hank doesn't come to family functions for a reason. Or maybe not. Maybe he's just worried and it would be okay after all."

Vince frowned at her. "What do you mean?"

Rachel gave him an incredulous look. "Hank's gay, Vinnie."

She might as well have thrown ice water on Vince. "He's what? Since when?"

"Birth, I suspect." She glanced sideways at Vince and smiled apologetically. "Or not. I don't know. But he is now. I thought you knew."

You don't want to end up like Hank. Vince put his cigarette to his lips. "Jesus."

"Not everyone knows. I think a lot of them are in denial."

"So the precedent here is, if you're gay, hide it?"

She sighed. "Maybe? But that doesn't mean you can't change it."

"Rach, I don't even know what I am. I mean, I don't feel gay."

"But you like Trey."

He nodded. "A lot. So I guess I am."

"Does it have to have a label? You can be bi or whatever. Or you can just be Vinnie. Trey's a good guy. If he makes you happy and you make him happy, go for it. Adopt a pile of kids if you want to be a good Fierro, or have a surrogate mother or something." When Vince twitched, she laughed. "Not ready for kids yet?"

"Fuck, no." Except the jolt hadn't been revulsion. More like a shock to his spinal cord at the idea of herding his own band of Fierros into a family event with Trey as his co-bouncer. Trey as part of his family. Trey, period.

No. It hadn't been revulsion at all.

He flicked the end of his cigarette into the alley. When Rachel handed him a second one, he took it.

"So you guys really aren't doing it?" she asked as he passed the lighter back. "I thought that was the gay perk or something: fucking like bunnies."

"Rachel, for God's sake." He grimaced at her. "Trey's not like that."

"Trey doesn't like sex?"

"Trey wants to wait for sex. Which I find charming." *And more than a bit of a relief.*

"So you didn't do *anything*?"

"Jesus. You want me to take a video the next time we make out, or what?"

Her eyes danced. "Yeah, that'd be all right."

Vince shivered. "*Rach.*"

She laughed. "Seriously, I'm glad it's working out. You seem happier. Nervous, but happy. Lose the nervous and I think this could be a great deal you have going."

"A great deal I can't bring home to the family."

"You don't know that."

He tipped his head back until it rested on the brick behind him. "I don't know either way."

"Well, just ride the ride until you're ready to try and find out." She elbowed him lightly. "And when you are, give me a holler, and I'll come play back up."

Vince's heart warmed at that, and he slid an arm around her before kissing her hair. "Thanks."

She kissed him back. "What else is family for?"

Chapter Fourteen

I'd gotten up early on Saturday for my shift at Full Moon, and the rest of the day was spent on homework until I got called in for someone sick at The Rose. Sunday was my day off from both places, and again, I spent the morning sequestered in my room, studying. When I came downstairs, I found my mother in the kitchen. She'd been drinking, but not too heavily, I could tell. She was in the happy stage. She hadn't started slurring or stumbling. Yet.

"I thought I'd make chicken parmesan for dinner tonight," she said to me. She wasn't looking at me. She was rifling through the open refrigerator.

"I won't be here, Mom. I'm going out."

"Again?" She closed the refrigerator door and turned to me. "I've barely seen you all week."

That was true, of course. I did my best to avoid her when she was drinking. "Sorry," I said, although I wasn't. "I made plans."

"But I'm making dinner."

"I'm sorry, Mom. I didn't know."

"What do I do now?" she asked. "Sit here alone? I'm completely alone, all the time, and neither of you even care."

"You're being overly dramatic, Mom. I have a date, that's all."

"You always have a date."

"That's not true. I don't go out that often and you know it."

"It's not fair, Trey. I'm here all day every day. The least you could do is keep me company."

"What? While you get drunk?" It was a low blow, but I'd long since grown tired of the kid gloves.

"What else am I supposed to do? You leave. Sophia goes to bed. You both leave me here by myself."

Of course she'd blame us. It was always somebody else's fault when she drank. She couldn't ever take responsibility for it herself.

I didn't bother trying to argue. Knowing she'd take it out on Gram, though, I went into the living room to try and tidy up a bit before she got home. She'd found some part-time work at the local grocery, which I didn't like because it was too much bending and too many idiots giving her a hard time, but she wouldn't say no, and it wasn't like we didn't need the money. I couldn't stop her from working, but I could try to make her life easier when she came back.

I'd picked up all the random clutter and trash and was about to run the vacuum when I remembered the bottle I'd kicked underneath the couch several days earlier. Saying a swift prayer I didn't find anything requiring an exterminator, I slid the sofa out into the middle of the room so I could retrieve the bottle and whatever else was underneath.

There weren't any bugs, but there wasn't one lone brown bottle, either. There were at least ten. My heart sank so far down into my stomach that it ached, even before I crouched down to pick one of them up. I knew what these were. I knew why they'd been tucked under the couch. I was pretty sure if I moved the chair where Mom usually sat, I'd find even more.

Cough syrup. Mom wasn't just drinking again. She was back on the goddamned cough syrup.

The first time she'd done this, it had taken me forever to understand why the hell someone would try and get high off of cough syrup. I hadn't even known it was possible. Back then I'd still been going to Al-Anon, the support group for families of alcoholics, and one of the counselors had tried to explain to me. Something about some chemical that gave the user euphoria. In medicinal doses it wasn't much noticeable, but sometimes people accidentally OD'd and figured it out, and if they were inclined to addiction, off they went. Personally I wondered if she hadn't heard about it that first time we'd sent her to rehab. Certainly she hadn't learned how to stop fucking herself over and us in the process.

I stared at the bottles, the old rage coming back over me like a tailor-made coat. My whole life had been like this, finding stashes of empty bottles in drawers and cupboards, in bags, more than once in the trunk of the car back when we still had one. Hidden, but not very damn well. I would almost have preferred it if she'd left them out in the open as some sort of defiance. In my younger days I'd have allowed myself to believe the therapists' crap that it was a cry for help, but I knew now what bullshit that really was. She didn't want help. She wanted an excuse to check out. If she'd wanted help, she'd have taken it when Gram had cashed in her retirement and sent her to the first treatment center. Or she'd have taken the help when Gram had sent her to the even more expensive center the second time, when she'd mortgaged the house. Or the third time, the place that had seemed more like a resort than anything, when we'd put up my college money and Gram had taken out the second mortgage.

All that money, and the longest it had ever lasted had been six months. That had been after the first center, and we'd had six months of believing maybe it was real. Maybe she was cured. But there was no cure. I understood that after the second center, and by the third one, I knew better than to hope at all. Good thing too, because she was drunk again less than three days after we brought her home.

So much for help. She didn't want it, and she didn't give a damn about what we thought, or what we gave up for her. She wanted to pout and complain about how hard it was to have her *disease.* She didn't care what it cost us or that it hurt us. She didn't care that Gram was working at a job that aggravated her arthritis just to make ends meet, because every penny she'd put away for retirement during her working years had been flushed down the treatment toilet. None of that mattered to my mom. *We* didn't matter.

But it mattered to me. Stealing money from Gram's purse and buying Lucky's out of cough syrup and vodka? Oh yeah, that mattered a lot. More than anything else in the world.

I dropped the bottle, stood, and shoved the couch back against the wall. The carpet wasn't vacuumed, but I didn't dare stay now, not with how mad I was. I'd end up in a fight with Mom, which wouldn't do a damn thing except make her pout and whine and be more of a mess for Gram.

She wasn't even Gram's daughter. Gram shouldn't have to do anything for her at all. She only did it for me, because if she didn't deal with it, I'd have to.

Mom called to me from the kitchen, and I ran out the front door before she could catch me.

I wished to hell I wasn't ever coming back.

I took the EL to Vin's house, chasing away the darkness finding the cough-syrup bottles had spawned by remembering my last date with Vin, how he'd been so nice, how he'd been so protective and gallant, and best of all, how he'd kissed me. By the time I got to his building, my stomach was full of butterflies. I couldn't stop myself from grinning like a fool while I waited for him to answer his door.

This time at least he wasn't dressed to the nines. Jeans, and a shirt, open at the collar and untucked. It was nice to see I wasn't the only one sporting a goofy grin. He had one to match.

"Hey," he said when he opened the door. "I'm almost ready. Come on in. I have to do one more thing."

I waited by the door while he disappeared down the hall,

doing what, I had no idea. While I hadn't expected anything specific about Vin's place, it still surprised me, and since I had nothing else to do, I tried to figure out why. In the end I decided I hadn't expected something so impersonal. It wasn't a man cave, full of beer bottles and sports magazines. It wasn't a mess, but it wasn't noticeably neat, either. Vin's place was...plain. Brown couch, brown chair, one end table. The kitchen was dull and serviceable, boasting the standard appliances and nothing else. Mail littered the table. The remote sat on the arm of his recliner. No plants, though. No fish tank. No posters. No decorations at all.

The only thing with any personality was the fridge, which was full top to bottom with pictures of Fierro children. I couldn't say why, but for some reason it made me sad.

Vince emerged from his bedroom, tugging a gold watch at his wrist. He'd put the gold chain back on too. "I thought we'd take my car. We can use the underground lot by Grant Park. You okay walking that far?"

"Of course."

He moved closer, backing me up against the door. He brushed my cheek with his fingertips. My heart felt like it might go into overdrive. "Can I kiss you again?"

I didn't answer with words. Instead, I stood on my toes, put my arms around his neck and welcomed him.

Our two kisses last time had been opposites—one frantic and sexy as hell, the other tame and sweet. This one was somewhere in between but left me as breathless as those had. I suddenly didn't give a damn about the aquarium.

"We should probably go," I said. Not because I wanted to, but because I *didn't* want to, and that scared me. I had a feeling he felt the same way.

"I think you're right."

He talked about his family in the car. He'd been at some kind of party the day before. There were so many of them. I spent most of the drive trying to sort out who he was talking about. We parked in the underground lot and meandered our way onto the craziness that was Michigan Avenue.

"The pizza place is right over there." He pointed up the street. "You hungry?"

"Not yet. Let's do the aquarium first."

"You got it."

It was a bright, warm, sunny day. The wind off the lake was cool and brisk, as always. The cries of the seagulls drifted around us. I wanted to hold his hand, or to snuggle against him as we walked and feel his arm around me, but I wasn't sure that was allowed. I moved a bit closer, letting our arms brush as we walked. He smiled over at me but didn't reach for me.

I was a little nervous about the entrance fee to the aquarium. Vinnie had paid for our last date, so I felt it was my turn. At the same time, there was no way I could afford to pay for us both. I decided the obvious answer was to buy my own ticket in and hope he wasn't bothered by the fact I hadn't paid his way too.

I made sure I reached the ticket counter ahead of him, but just as I was saying, "One, please," he wrapped his arm around my waist and pulled me away from the counter.

"What are you doing?" he teased. "This is a date, remember? You think we're going stag?"

I felt myself blush. "You paid on Monday—"

"So?"

"It's only fair."

He laughed. "I'll tell you what, if you're worried about fair, I'll let you buy the pizza."

The aquarium was crowded as hell, but still fun. At first Vin acted nervous, looking around to see if people were watching us. Of course they weren't. Not with the massive displays of exotic fish all around us. The nice thing about the crowd was that we had a perfectly good excuse to stand extra close. When I leaned into him, I thought he liked it. He seemed to welcome the contact.

We were in the midst of so many people, and yet all I could see was him. He was fun, and sexy, and flirtatious. He eclipsed everything. I barely even noticed the amazing displays around us. I wanted only to be close to him, and although I felt I was being foolish and rather obvious, I couldn't help it. Each casual touch or fleeting caress lit me and warmed me from the inside. I spent each moment longing for the next contact.

"How about that pizza now?" he finally asked.

I checked my watch. We'd been wandering around the aquarium for over three hours. I hadn't quite realized I was hungry, but his mention of pizza made my stomach growl.

"Sounds good."

The walk back to the park and down the street to the pizza place was better. He put his arm over my shoulders. That spot against his side felt like it was made just for me. He felt so big and strong, and he smelled amazing. Even though I was hungry, I was a bit disappointed when we reached the restaurant, because it meant moving away from him.

I was halfway through my first piece of pizza when he asked, "How about a movie after dinner?"

I died a little inside when I had to say, "I can't."

"C'mon." Under the table, he nudged my foot playfully with his. "I'll even let you pick. Any movie you want."

It was tempting. Two hours in a dark room. In public, so sex wouldn't be too much of a temptation, but plenty of opportunity for snuggling close and holding his hand. But then I thought about the unfinished homework waiting for me at home, and the fact that my alarm would be going off at 4:30 the next morning.

Would I be able to work, though, knowing I could be off somewhere with Vin, making out like a teenager? Would I ever be able to sleep?

Maybe after the movie he'd talk me into going back to his place.

Maybe I could call in sick to work, or beg Sara to go in for me, if I promised to work next Sunday for her.

I was almost ready to cave and tell him I'd do it when my phone rang. I pulled it out of my pocket and looked at the screen, and my heart fell. It was my home number. There were two possibilities. The first was that it was my mother calling to lay some kind of guilt trip on me. The second was that it was my grandmother, and she wouldn't call unless it was an emergency. Neither outcome was going to be good.

"Hello?"

"Trey, it's me," Gram said. "Your mom's in the hospital."

Cough syrup.

My grandmother was still talking, telling me the details, but it didn't matter. I knew the score. We'd done this before, hadn't we? Just like the rehab, just like everything else. We'd even done cough syrup hospitalization before. They'd told her she wasn't supposed to mix it with Cymbalta, but did she listen? No. Because it wasn't what she wanted to hear.

Forget homework. Forget work in the morning. Absolutely forget making out with Vinnie, because Mom had decided that, once again, the whole goddamned world was about her and her *disease.*

Something inside of me rebelled. Some little piece of me wanted to scream in rage. There are only so many emergencies a person can take before the urgency turns to weariness. Only so many blackouts and trips to the emergency room. Only so many rehab waiting rooms or tearful promises that this will be the last time. At some point, every new drama was just another trip around the carousel.

I was so goddamned tired of riding this ride.

When I hung up the phone, I tried to avoid looking in Vinnie's eyes. "I have to go. My mom's in the hospital."

Oh, but I hated the concern on his face most of all. "Is she okay?" He was already standing up, tossing bills onto the table. "I can take you—"

"No!" I didn't want any of this to happen, but I certainly didn't want Vin in the middle of my family drama. I didn't want him to know the details of our sordid lives. If Vin and I kept dating, he'd find out eventually, but I wanted to put it off a bit longer.

"It's okay," I told him, trying to sound calm. "I'll grab the EL—"

His expression became stormy, and all of a sudden I had a big, angry, overprotective Fierro bearing down on me. "Trey, don't be ridiculous. My car is right around the corner. Let's go."

Vinnie touched my shoulder, squeezing it briefly in reassurance, and headed for the door.

The only thing I could really do was follow.

Chapter Fifteen

All the way to the hospital, Trey was silent, which did nothing to help Vince figure out how to respond. He had no idea what Trey needed. Support, yes, but what kind? If this were his family, everyone would be a melted mess, and he'd buck up and be strong. But Trey made hardwood look limber and pliant. He wasn't stoic, but he wasn't exactly despondent. It was almost eerie, his reaction. It didn't fit in any way with what Vince thought of as the buffet of choices when the main course was *my mother has been taken to the hospital and whisked into the emergency room*. Not despair, not indifference. Just this weird wall and tension all the way to the hospital, and it only escalated once they were in the waiting room.

Sophia was already there, holding a magnifying glass and a *Reader's Digest*. She had a companion expression to Trey's, though there was a weariness to her that seemed to fit better. When she saw her grandson, her whole demeanor changed, and she motioned him over. He let her embrace him and kissed her cheek, but Vince noticed Trey never relaxed, not even with her.

They didn't talk. Trey didn't ask what was wrong, just looked at his grandmother with a silent question, and Sophia responded with a curt nod, as if to say, *Yes, it's what you think*.

Trey's response was to turn away.

No one explained to Vince what had happened or why Mindy was admitted. Instinct warned Vince not to ask.

It was one of the hardest evenings of Vince's life, though for the strangest reasons. He wanted to be there for Trey like he wanted little else, but it was eight kinds of hell trying to figure out what *being there* looked like. The need to talk to Trey, to get *him* to talk, was a pulsing urgency, but Vince couldn't tell if that was instinct or habit because that was what he was used to. With his family, if he went along to the hospital with his brother and a sick kid, he knew his job, and that was to listen to people vent, to get them to a safe space where they could fall apart.

Vince couldn't tell what the hell his job was here. Worse yet, he wasn't sure if Trey wanted him there, not at first. After swallowing several, *You okays*, Vince was all set to point-blank ask if Trey wanted him to stay when all of a sudden Trey leaned against his shoulder.

Okay. Vince let out a quiet breath of relief. *Finally.* He had a fucking job to do.

He glanced around the waiting room. They were seated in a row of chairs with god-awful uncomfortable armrests between them, which meant that even if he could disengage his arm to wrap it around Trey, he'd only mash them up against a metal bar. Almost as a gift from God, though, a couple rose from one of the few comfortable seating offerings, this one a small sofa that promised its occupants if not a nap at least a moment of potential repose.

Gently dislodging Trey, Vince rose. When Trey didn't reach for his offered hand, he bent and took Trey's palm and hauled him up as well, launching them both across the room at a decent clip.

"What?" was all Trey managed before Vince pushed him down by the shoulders into the couch.

"You want anything?" He kept hold of Trey's hand, but he didn't sit. "Something to eat? Drink? Read? Throw?"

He did a mental fist pump when the last one made a tiny smile flirt with Trey's mouth. "I'd love a Sprite." Looking up at Vince, Trey squeezed his hand. "Thanks."

Vince winked at him and squeezed back. "Save my spot."

A bit of wandering found him a gift shop, where he bought not only the biggest Sprite they had but two bags of snack mix and a couple of word search and crossword books, as well as a pack of mechanical pencils. He stopped by the cafe and got a hot tea with lemon for Sophia and a black coffee for himself and headed back to the waiting room. Sophia accepted the tea with a grateful if not sad smile and continued staring at the *Reader's Digest* in her lap. Vince was sure she hadn't actually opened it yet.

Trey had moved to the very edge of the couch and seemed poised to take flight at any given second, but when he saw Vince, he eased back into the couch. He accepted the Sprite with a quiet murmur of thanks, and when Vince tilted the open bag of snack mix for him, Trey ate a little.

Vince put his arm around Trey's back and rubbed at his shoulders, opening up a space against the side of his own body. Trey slid into him like he was coming home.

Vince shut his eyes before he could glance nervously around to see who watched and what they thought, making damn sure this moment was only for and all about Trey. He was a big, burly Italian, and he wasn't stupid: it felt good to lean against a big Italian man. He remembered quite well how good it had felt as a boy to curl up against his father, and if he didn't miss his guess, Trey was feeling more than a bit of his inner little boy right now. Vince kept his arm around Trey's shoulders, ran his fingers in reassuring circles over his sleeve, and pressed his lips into Trey's soft, fragrant hair in between sips of his coffee to keep himself from murmuring stupid platitudes to fill the silence.

He'd just started a word find and was about to entice Trey into joining him when Sophia suddenly sat up straight, her body abruptly taut with tension. Seeing her, Trey tensed as well.

Vince squeezed his arm reassuringly as a doctor in scrubs came toward them. Trey made no response, only went more rigid.

The doctor smiled one of those weirdly placid doctor smiles. "She's going to be okay."

There was a strange pause, and both Vince and the doctor glanced back and forth, waiting for the sigh of relief, the tears of gratitude, the *thank Gods* and all the usuals. But like everything else about this, Vince didn't get what he expected. Sophia shut her eyes for a long moment, then turned to Trey, who deflated in what Vince at first thought was release, but when those blue eyes lifted, all Vince could see was despair. Once again Sophia seemed to know what Vince did not, namely what was going on inside Trey's head.

It was starting to drive Vince crazy. He wanted *in*. He wanted to find out why Trey looked so shut off and dead and helpless, and he wanted to fucking fix it.

He was *going* to fucking fix it.

He leaned closer to Trey, rubbing circles against his back. "Trey, baby, tell me what you need."

Without moving his gaze from his grandmother's, Trey said, his voice dull and flat, "I want to go home."

"Okay," Vince replied. "Do you want to see your mom first?"

"No. I just want to go home." Trey turned to look at him, his gaze still flat and dead. "Can you take us home?"

"Of course."

The eerie silence continued as they left the hospital. Trey only broke it once, long enough to argue with Sophia over who should sit in the front seat. "Don't be silly," Sophia said at last. "Vinnie doesn't want to talk to me all the way home." And so she'd taken the backseat, and Trey took the front, but despite Sophia's words, it didn't really matter who Vince wanted to talk to. It was obvious Trey had no desire to talk at all. He sat, silent and stoic, leaning against the window with his eyes closed.

Sophia seemed to have recovered from whatever had happened at the hospital. "How's Frank?" she asked.

"Good. Proud of his grandbabies, as ever."

"He's such a good man. He always was."

Vince caught a glimpse of her in the rearview mirror, surprised at the wistfulness he saw in her features. And loneliness.

An idea struck him, and he went with it. "You should stop by and see him more often. He gets awful lonely, I think, with everyone gone. With his rheumatism, he can't babysit like he wants, either."

It felt good to see the soft smile play at Sophia's lips. "I just might do that."

Despite his victory in the car, Vince was back to being unsure of what to do when they reached the house. Trey was barely looking at him, and Vince didn't know how to ask if he should stay or leave.

Luckily, Sophia stepped in then, as well. "Come in," she said. "He wants you here."

"Are you sure?" he asked. Trey was already at the front door, unlocking it, seemingly unaware of the conversation going on at the curb.

Sophia patted his arm. "My Trey has a big heart. When he's happy, he could lift us all up to the clouds, but when he's down, it's hard for him to find his way out of the dark."

The words were like tumblers in a lock falling into place, and Vince stared at Trey's back as the revelation settled in. God, how had he missed it? Trey was like Rachel. When things really upset her, she shut everyone out, and almost everybody went. Only Vince had ever figured out how to help her, to simply be present and give her space enough to come apart. He'd bet money Trey came apart the same way too, not in big sobs or dramatic fits but in subtle sighs. He thought of how Trey had melted into him at the hospital, and he didn't just think he was right. He knew it.

He followed Sophia inside, and he thought maybe he did

111

see a hint of relief in Trey's blue eyes. "I'm going to bed," Sophia said immediately. She shook her finger at Vince. "And don't you worry. Once my hearing aid's out, I can't hear a thing."

Vince felt his ears begin to burn at her implication, but he was happy to see a ghost of a smile on Trey's lips. But then Sophia was gone, and it was the two of them, staring at each other. Vince suddenly felt awkward.

"Thank you," Trey said at last.

"I didn't do much." In truth, he was still frustrated he hadn't been able to do more. "Is there anything you need?"

Trey looked away, biting his lip hesitantly. "Will you stay for a bit? Sit with me?"

Yep. Rachel all over again. Vince smiled. "Anything."

Trey led him to the couch. Vince sat, and Trey instantly curled up against him as he had at the hospital. Vince leaned back, turning toward Trey so he could wrap his arms around him and hold him close.

"I don't want to think for awhile," Trey whispered.

There were a few ways Vince could accomplish that. Holding him as close as he was, the memory of their dance and their kiss still so fresh in his mind, he had some very good ideas about how to distract Trey. But he knew now wasn't the time.

He reached out and grabbed the remote off the coffee table. He turned on the TV and began flipping through channels. "Tell me when to stop."

After a few minutes, Trey said, "Here."

It was Marilyn Monroe—*The Seven Year Itch*, if Vince remembered his old movies right.

Trey snuggled closer. For a long time, he was completely silent. Then he let out a long, shuddering breath.

"Champagne and potato chips," he mumbled. Vince thought maybe the ice was breaking. Maybe this was when Trey would let everything out.

However, when he looked down at the boy in his arms, he found that Trey was fast asleep.

Chapter Sixteen

The hospital kept my mom overnight. "For observation," they said. They also hinted, none too lightly, that with the amount of cough syrup and vodka she'd consumed, they suspected she'd been trying to commit suicide.

I refused to let myself think about that.

When my phone alarm went off, I got up and went to work my shift at the coffee shop, dead on my feet, then walked to campus for my classes. I tried not to think about my mother, but it was impossible.

Things like this had happened in the past, and always the question was, had she done it on purpose? A few of the times, the overdoses had been legitimate accidents. Some of the others? Maybe not. Had this time been a serious attempt, or just another *cry for attention*? It was possible I'd never know.

Did it matter?

Did I care anymore?

Did it make me a bad person if I didn't?

I tried instead to think about Vinnie, who had stayed with me for half the night while I dozed in the warmth of his arms. He'd promised to call me later, and I clung to that vow, the only bright moment ahead of me.

It was shortly after noon when he called. "I wanted to see how you're doing."

"I'm fine," I lied. Before he could ask about my mom, I said, "Thanks so much, Vinnie."

"No need to thank me."

"Well, still."

"Is there anything you need?"

"No. No, I'm fine."

"Well, at least let me take you out for pizza, since we never got to finish our date last night."

Our date.

I wanted to say yes, but there was no way in the world I could take him up on the offer. I still had a shift to cover at the restaurant, plus a paper to write when I got home, and another early shift at the coffee shop the next day. "I have way too much homework, Vin. I'm sorry."

"Don't apologize. Just tell me when I can see you again."

Was it pathetic how much the protectiveness in his voice made me melt? I actually found myself smiling. "I have Thursday off."

"Thursday it is. I think it's well past time we got the fountain out of the way."

My smile hurt my face it was so big. "Probably so."

"Call me whenever you want, okay? No matter if it's day or night."

"I will."

"Promise me you will."

I could fall in love with him, I realized. I really could. Maybe I was already there. "I promise."

By the time I got back to my house after work that night, my mom was home from the hospital. She was on the couch, wrapped in a blanket, a cup of tea in her hand. She was in full apology mode.

I braced myself, knowing I didn't dare buy one word of it.

"Trey, I'm so sorry—"

"Save it."

"It won't happen again. I promise."

"I don't want your goddamn promises. You never keep them anyway."

"Honey, I was just so lonely. And I'd had a bit to drink—"

"No kidding."

"—and I must have taken my pills earlier in the day, but I forgot, and I guess I took them again. I don't know—"

"Mom, forget it, all right?" I turned at the foot of the stairs to face her. "You're sorry. I'm sorry. Gram's sorry. We all know how it goes."

She hung her head. "I didn't remember taking them."

She looked so old, and so beaten. She had so little. A couch. A TV. A bottle. Lots and lots of bottles. Everything else was gone. Granted, outside of my father's death, it was all gone because of her drinking. It was her own fault.

That didn't make this single moment any easier.

I felt a hint of something—something I hadn't felt for her in a long time—a hint of sympathy.

Once upon a time, things had been different. She'd been drinking then too, but I'd been too young to understand. All I'd known then was that some days she was confused and clumsy. On the other days, she was my friend.

I'd told Vinnie how she'd taught me to aim for the 100s in skee-ball. At least once a week we'd go to Orecchio's to play, or go out for ice cream, or maybe go to a movie. Back then, she'd tried so hard to make up for the fact that my dad wasn't around. But as I got older, the drinking got worse. She became more of a hermit too.

In those days, I'd wanted to understand, but she began to embarrass me more often than not. She'd show up drunk at my school events. Back then she'd had a job, and more than once, her boss had called me to come and get her because she'd gone to work drunk. Of course, she ended up being fired.

That had been a turning point. Even in high school, I'd

worked part-time. My grandmother hung on to her job as a secretary at the junior high for as long as she could. She could take shorthand and had designed their entire filing system. The problem was, those skills were no longer needed. After forty-five years of work, they looked at her as nothing but a dinosaur who couldn't understand how to use a computer. They'd forced her into retirement only three months before my mom lost her job. Suddenly, working part-time wasn't enough. I was the sole breadwinner in the family.

My mom had other jobs after that, but none of them ever lasted. The drinking became a daily thing. I was seventeen the first time she ended up in the hospital.

I'd thought maybe it was my fault.

I'd thought I could help her or change her.

Of course, I'd learned Al-Anon's three Cs later: I didn't cause it, I can't control it, I can't cure it. Coddling, threatening, bargaining, begging. None of them worked.

Neither did anger or indifference. That was the part I struggled with.

She was still on the couch, crying quietly. I couldn't control her, no.

But I could control me.

"Do you still have the stuff for chicken parmesan?"

She looked up at me, her eyes red and swollen. "Yes."

"I need to write a paper, but I really am hungry."

She smiled at me, and I tried to tell myself it was worth it. "I'll call you down when it's ready."

Chapter Seventeen

For the next few weeks, Vince found ample reasons to drop by Little Italy, particularly Loomis Street.

He texted Trey a lot, but he found those brief messages unsatisfying. *I'm fine,* Trey would text back, but those cold, impersonal letters on the screen of his phone felt empty. There was no tone, no way to look into Trey's eyes to judge the depth of the lie. Instead, Vince took to seeing for himself. He couldn't bring himself to go to The Rose, but he developed a severe early-morning latte habit, taking the EL down to Full Moon before heading up to Northbrook. It meant he was getting up almost as early as Trey, but it was worth it to see him every morning, to make sure he was okay.

Trey wasn't at the house all the time when Vince stopped by, either off studying or working, but that didn't bother him. He liked to sit in the kitchen with Sophia, chatting about his family, letting her reminisce about old times, urging her to go visit Frank at his bar. Every now and again he got her to go too, promising to mind her dinner in the oven and doing little fix-it jobs around the house. After he de-clogged the upstairs sink drain, he messed with the leaky pipe under the kitchen basin and bought new guts for the first-floor toilet so it didn't run all the damn time. The fluorescent light in the basement laundry was next, and the bulb in the fussy fixture over the stair landing.

When he fixed the front porch steps, though, Trey gave him hell. He'd gotten the job done before Trey came back from work, but there was no mistaking the fact that he'd gone out and bought new treads, which was apparently well over the line.

He'd bought new risers too, but Trey hadn't noticed those, so he didn't share that bit of information.

"You can't do that," Trey protested. "You can't just show up and buy us new stairs. And don't give me that eyebrow either."

Vince hadn't realized he'd been giving eyebrow. He carefully schooled his expression. "Why can't I fix your stairs?"

"Because you can't."

"I did," Vince pointed out.

Trey's ears were red, from anger or embarrassment, Vince couldn't tell. "It's too much. You shouldn't have done it."

"I'm pretty sure they weren't up to code, and I've seen Sophia almost trip on them twice. It's not a big deal. I've installed more stairs than I have pipes." He gave Trey a sideways grin. "Did a stint in construction for my other uncle."

Trey didn't stop frowning, but he seemed to give in all the same. "Well, you still shouldn't have, but thank you. Don't think I haven't noticed everything else you've been doing around the house, either. And is it my imagination, or are you trying to set Gram up with Frank?"

"Yeah. Don't know if it will take, but I figured why not, can't hurt anything."

He loved the way Trey softened and came closer to him. "Is this your way of trying to get into my pants?"

Vince couldn't tell if Trey was teasing or not. He suspected it was a mix, but he answered with complete honesty. "No, it's my way of taking care of you. Though I wouldn't say no to your pants, either."

Trey smiled and punched him lightly in the arm, but he caught Vince's hand and led him back inside.

Those wicked websites had become a regular feature in Vince's evenings, and he was starting to make a mental list of things he wanted to try. He'd found a chat room too, which had been all kinds of education, and actually, a hell of a lot of therapy. It turned out he wasn't the only almost-forty-year-old who'd worked like hell to tell himself he was straight and ended up figuring his shit out in the fifth inning. The chat room was a safe place to ask embarrassing questions, like how, exactly, did he go about having gay sex, because he hadn't missed the creative cuts in the porn he'd watched. He'd learned more about lube than he'd thought there was to know about the stuff. He'd bought some too, and the last couple of times he'd masturbated, he'd started experimenting with his own ass. It was weird at first. Back when he'd fooled around in college, anal play had equaled gay in his mind. As long as he stayed away from that, he could call himself straight. Of course he knew enough now to know that enjoying anal contact had nothing to do with being gay or straight. It only had to do with being able to relax enough to enjoy it.

It was something he was learning to do rather quickly. He'd even bought a small dildo online although he hadn't found the nerve yet to use it. He wasn't sure he could tell Trey about that.

He wanted to, though. He wanted to tell Trey everything.

He wanted Trey to use that dildo on him. He wanted Trey to do a lot of things to him.

Except he was still scared out of his mind.

Mindy was in the living room when they came inside, watching television and swaying lightly from side to side. One glance in her direction had all the tension back in Trey's shoulders.

Vince put his hand on them, massaging gently. "What do you say we go upstairs and neck in your room like a couple of kids?" he whispered into Trey's ear.

As he'd hoped, this made Trey smile and lead him up the stairs.

Once inside, though, Trey made no move to make out, only began to pace in agitation in the space between his desk and his closet, and Vince sat on the bed, ready to listen to the frustration he knew was about to pour out. He didn't have to wait long.

"My mom's an alcoholic."

Just like that. No preamble. No sugarcoating it. Vince did his best to look unsurprised.

"She's been drinking again. Not long ago she drank so much she almost died, and now she's back at it. God. I just want to pound something." Trey shoved a hand into his hair, messing it up, tightening his fingers inside the golden strands. Vince kept still, waiting, and Trey eventually went on. "I hate that you know."

That one threw Vince. "Why? Did you think I was going to be a dick about it? Didn't you think I'd want to help you?"

Trey's cheeks colored as his rage simmered up to boiling. "I don't *want* help. I don't want to have to *need* help. I want to be normal. I won't be, though, not until—" His face became a mask, and he turned away from Vince.

Normal. Vince wanted to laugh. Yeah, didn't they all? And wasn't he a dick, worried about what people thought about him dating a guy and looking up gay sex on the net—how that wasn't normal. For Trey that was fine. He only wanted to have a mom who wasn't on the bottle.

"Has she tried AA? Or—"

"God, yes. Of course, although not for years. I did it too, for awhile. Al-Anon, you know. The part for families? But it just pissed me off more. Here she was, sitting at home getting wasted, and I was the one trying to work meetings into my schedule, memorizing the twelve steps and reciting the serenity prayer and trying to accept that there's a fucking 'higher power'." He laughed bitterly. "What they don't tell you is that God has nothing to do with it. Alcohol is their 'higher power'."

"Honey, I'm so sorry."

"What I hate most," Trey went on as if Vince hadn't spoken, gripping his desk chair and staring out the window as he spoke, "is how she uses it as her excuse. I know she was upset when my dad died. I know it was hard as hell on her. I found out a few years ago she was on pills even before that, but Dad getting shot only made things worse. She went from a little bit depressed to complete basket case. They gave her Valium like it was candy. The year I was born they came out with Prozac, but her doctor was old school and didn't like it. They finally got her onto it when I was in middle school, but it was too late, I think. She was popping pills constantly. And drinking. And by then she was so agoraphobic she couldn't go anywhere unless she was drunk or high. Not even the grocery store or the mall."

Jesus. "You mean she got drunk, hopped on the EL and got her groceries?"

Trey's laugh was so brittle it nearly broke in half. "Are you kidding? She drove. If we had a car, she'd still drive, but we sold that years ago. This was after she'd been fired the last time, and Gram had told her she had to start helping around the house—getting groceries and running errands. So Mom would wait for me to come home from school, and then she'd drive us to the liquor store. She'd down three cans in the parking lot so we could go buy stuff for dinner or get me the new sweats I needed for gym class. The crazy thing is, I didn't realize then how fucked up that was. I only knew I was embarrassed about being at the mall with my mom stumbling up and down through the shops. And then I'd feel guilty for—"

Vince couldn't take it anymore. He stood and took Trey's arm, forcing the boy to turn and face him.

"What?" Trey asked in confusion.

What? Did he really need to ask that? Vince couldn't get past his disbelief and his rage enough to speak. He wanted to accuse Trey of making the whole thing up, but he could tell he wasn't. He was being forced to see Mindy in a whole new light, and it wasn't pretty. He had the urge to go downstairs and scream at her, ask her how she could have done something so selfish.

"You're shaking," Trey said, sounding more confused than ever. He took Vince's hands, stilling them, and at last Vince found his voice.

"You have got to be shitting me. She *waited for you* so she could fucking drunk-drive you around Chicago?"

"She worried she'd have a panic attack, and she figured I could drive her home in an emergency."

"Jesus Fucking Christ! How old were you?"

Trey seemed confused about where Vin was going. "I don't know. Thirteen. Fourteen, maybe?"

"What about a goddamned cab?"

"They were too expensive. Besides, then people would know." Trey blinked, looking almost wary. "Vinnie, why are you so mad?"

"Why am I mad? Fucking hell, Trey. I'm mad because your mom put you through that in goddamned *middle school*. I can't believe your Gram let her do that!"

Now Trey was defensive. "Gram has nothing to do with it. She didn't know."

"That doesn't make it any better. You shouldn't have had to do that. *Nobody* should have to do that, ever, but you damn well shouldn't have been your mother's back-up plan when you were barely a teenager."

He thought his rage would make Trey feel better. That it would somehow validate Trey's own anger, but he'd be damned if Trey didn't retreat more every time Vince told him what he'd been through was wrong. "I was fine. I mean, it wasn't great—"

"It was fucking wrong in every way something can be wrong," Vince said, no room for argument in his tone. "I don't care that you got through it. Thank God you're as smart and strong as you are, but that doesn't make it any better. It shouldn't have happened."

"I'm not smart and strong, not really. And it wasn't that big of a deal. It wasn't more than I could handle."

What the hell was with him being so stubborn? "It wasn't what you deserved. It wasn't what you needed. If one of my siblings or cousins did something even half as bad as that, the family would be down on them so hard—"

"Don't you get it?" Trey was angry again, but there was hurt in his voice that wasn't there before. "I don't have family like that. I hardly have any family at all. I have Mom and Gram, and Gram was still grieving Grandpa and working full-time and trying to keep us—"

"*I don't care.*" Vince gripped Trey's shoulders, all but shaking him. "You deserved family. You deserved to be taken care of."

"I just told you, I didn't—"

"Why the hell won't you hear that you should have had help?" Vince all but roared at him. "Is it gonna break you in half or something if you admit you got a fucked-up deal, that you had to grow up too soon, that when someone should have been taking care of you, you were taking care of them instead?"

Trey didn't answer, but his nostrils flared, and his pale blue eyes filled with angry tears.

Too late Vince realized that yes, admitting it would break Trey in half, or at least break down the safe, protective walls of *I'm fine* he'd built up while he'd sat in that car watching his mom get herself blitzed. Admitting how fucked up that had been was almost worse than living through the shit in the first place. It was enough to have to deal with his drunk mother now, *today*, sitting on the couch downstairs. Dealing with an entire lifetime of hurt and disappointment wasn't even an option.

One day at a time. That was the saying, right?

Vince blew the last of his fury out as best he could and slid a hand up to cup the back of Trey's head. He massaged his hair as he searched for an apology, trying to acknowledge what he'd sussed out without exactly bringing it up. To tell him that maybe he'd been in a pile of shit all alone then, but he sure as hell wasn't now.

It turned out there weren't words for that sort of thing. Vince bent down and kissed him instead, a soft, sweet and lingering kiss across his lips.

Trey made a quiet choking sound that broke Vince's heart.

"I'm sorry," Vince whispered into Trey's hair. "I'm so sorry."

"I'm fine."

Vince almost laughed. Trey said those words so often, like a mantra, like by saying them enough, he could make them true. "What do you want me to do?" Vince asked.

Trey tilted his head back, and although his cheeks were red and his eyes moist, he smiled flirtatiously up at Vinnie. "How about if you distract me?"

Vince was happy to oblige.

He pulled Trey to the bed, kissing him gently, trying to comfort him, but it soon became clear Trey wasn't interested in being coddled. It was like someone had unleashed a wild animal, if a wild animal pressed people into beds and fucked them with their tongue while shoving their legs apart and grinding hard against their groins. Trey was several inches shorter than Vince and not nearly as big around, but he had pent-up rage and something else Vince couldn't quite identify coursing through him. Vince couldn't have gotten away from him that moment even if he wanted to.

Mother of God forgive him, but he didn't want to.

Vince went slack under Trey's assault, bearing him up so he didn't tip over, lifting his legs to create a cradle for his lover, but otherwise he lay there and let Trey have his way with him. Trey's kisses were so hard they were almost brutal, the kind of kisses Vince had dreamed about every time he'd seen Jimmy Valente in the locker-room shower in high school. Rough kisses full of teeth and thrusts that made him shiver and ache. Deep kisses that gave him goose bumps and made his cock swell against Trey's own.

God, but it felt like high school, like the wicked moments he'd had with girls when they'd snuck him into their bedrooms, except this time he felt like the girl. Actually, no. Those girls were almost vicious. Vince felt like the virginal shy flowers he'd been taught girls were. Vince felt like a vessel, an open place for all the emotions Trey was pouring into him. More than anything in the world, he wanted Trey to break the kiss, sit back on his dick and strip his shirt away. He wanted Trey to take his shirt off too, and his pants, and he wanted Trey to turn him over and—

He shut his eyes tight, not letting that line of thought go any further.

He focused on Trey's mouth instead, and his hands, and the incredibly sexy way his hips ground against Vince, making his cock so hard it hurt. Trey's cock was hard too, hard as a goddamned rock inside his jeans.

Vince wanted it in his mouth.

Trey suddenly broke their kiss, ducking his head into Vince's chest. "I'm sorry," he panted.

"Don't apologize. Just keep going."

Trey's cheeks were flushed. His lips were swollen and red. The naked arousal in his eyes was the sexiest thing Vince had ever seen. "I want to," Trey said. "I really do. But not here."

"Fair enough." Vince caught his bottom lip with his teeth, tugging on it gently. "Split the difference." When Trey looked down at him in lust-filled confusion, Vince winked. "We got first base down pat. Wanna try for second?"

Trey stared at him a moment longer. Then he smiled a wicked, beautiful smile and shoved Vince's shirt up to his armpits.

The first brush of Trey's fingers on his nipples made Vince suck in a breath and swell so hard against his zipper he thought he'd hurt himself. "Holy shit," he whispered, then cried out as Trey pulled gently on the taut nub of skin.

"Is this what you want?" Trey whispered, and tugged again.

Vince arched into his touch, precome dampening his briefs. "I want you to do whatever you want to do."

When Trey's mouth closed over his nipple, Vince bucked with so much force he almost knocked them off the bed. *Holy Mother of God.* He had no idea that could feel so good. A couple of girls had teased his nipples a little, but never like this. Nobody'd ever sucked him. He clutched at Trey's head, trying to keep him there, gasping and all but crying.

Trey licked around his areola, one of his hands trailing down Vince's stomach. "I want to touch you. I want to touch your cock."

Fear threatened to shut Vince down, but there was too much want, too much yearning. "I want to touch you too. I want to hold our cocks together in my hand and jack against you until we both come." The terror bit him sharp, but he pressed on. "I want to lick it all off your belly and suck you until you get hard in my mouth and come again."

Trey's fingers bit into Vince's side.

Then they traveled down, very insistently, to his fly.

The doorknob rattled. "Trey?" Sophia called through the wood.

Vince and Trey moved apart like they were on fire. Trey flashed him an apologetic, shaky smile. "Yeah, Gram?"

The doorknob rattled again, and the door opened. Vince tugged his shirt down and grabbed Trey's pillow, shoving it over his crotch.

Belatedly he realized this was about as dead a giveaway to what they'd been doing as he could give, but Sophia played it as cool as a cucumber. "Oh hello, Vincent. I was wondering if you were here, and I see you are. Should I set an extra place for dinner?"

Trey smiled at Vince, lust still banked in his gaze, and Vince nearly came in his pants.

"No—" Vince's voice cracked, and he cleared his throat. "No. I gotta get back." He had to get home and jerk the hell off, that's what. "But thank you."

"The steps look wonderful." Her eyes might have been twinkling. "You're certainly spoiling us around here, with all your projects." She glanced apologetically at Trey. "I was going to ask you to set the table, but I don't want to interrupt."

Christ. Vince stood, taking his pillow with him. "No. Really. I gotta get going. Really." He hesitated at Trey, then gave in and kissed him on the cheek. "I'll call you later."

He remembered halfway down the stairs to drop the pillow.

Chapter Eighteen

I hadn't told Josh, Tara or Dillon about Vin. I'd kept news of my relationship quiet in part because I didn't want to out Vince before he was ready, but mostly because of the sheer nosiness of my friends. They knew I was saving myself for "The One", and I wasn't ready to be interrogated on the state of my virginity.

I also didn't want to hear their opinions on the wisdom of teasing myself with a closeted man more than ten years my senior.

It couldn't stay a secret forever, though. Vinnie was around me so much, people had noticed. He was practically a Full Moon morning regular, and he might have been trying to be down-low about why he was there, but nobody bought it.

One day we all stopped by the shop together, and when Dillon was ordering and Josh and Tara were in some heated discussion beside me, Sara smiled at me over the espresso machine and said, "No boyfriend today?"

Josh and Tara went stone silent, and Dillon turned around to stare open-mouthed at me, his order forgotten.

"Shit," I swore, but the proverbial cat was out of the bag. There was no escape. They were ruthless. They blocked me into the corner and badgered me until I'd spilled the whole story.

"He's a good guy," I insisted when they made a face at how old he was and that he was still in the closet. "His family is amazing, which you already know—he's a Fierro."

"The restaurant," Josh said, looking impressed.

Tara wasn't so easy. "I don't care if he's from the fucking First Family and comes with the Good Housekeeping Seal. If he's using you, I'll kick his ass."

I wished Vin could see this. Family? Hell, I had it in spades. Whoever said blood was thicker than water hadn't met my friends.

It was Dillon who asked the question I'd been dreading. "So, have you done it yet?"

"Not that it's any of your business, but we haven't done anything." I thought of how he'd come apart in my arms when I'd sucked on his nipple and blushed. "Much."

"How come we haven't met him then?" he challenged. "Why are you letting him keep you as his dirty little secret?"

"You haven't met him because of how you're acting right now." Except I couldn't really be mad at them. Nuts as they were, I did love how protective they were being, and I kind of wanted to hug them all. "I'll talk to him about it, okay?"

Dillon and Josh looked mollified, but Tara still had her arms folded over her chest. "You've been ditching us for weeks. Do you have any idea how worried we've been? Dillon was all about giving you space, letting you come to us. I thought maybe your mom was bad again."

Now I felt guilty. "She is, actually. But that's not—" I sighed. "I didn't mean to ditch you. I'm sorry. I don't know what I was thinking."

Dillon snorted. "You weren't thinking. Not with your big head, anyway."

Tara whacked me on the arm, and I winced. "I'm sorry, I really am."

Josh smiled a soft, knowing kind of smile. "Ignore them. They're just sore because I was right. They thought something was wrong because you were acting funny. Smiling like a dork for no reason. Running into walls because you were checking your phone. Missing half of conversations because you were staring off into nothing." His smile grew wider. "I told them you were acting like someone in love."

I went still, Josh's words rushing down inside me like Luke Skywalker's fatal hit to the Death Star. I wanted to tell him no, he was crazy, I wasn't in love with Vincent Fierro.

But as Tara rolled her eyes and told me I was forgiven so long as I produced him for inspection within a week, as Dillon mock leered and teased me, promising to give me all the pointers I wanted on how to have sex, I thought about Vin and how he made me feel and all that Josh had said, and I realized he could be right. I might be in love with Vinnie. With the man who fixed my steps and held doors for me and brought Gram tea when we sat in the waiting room, who set her up with his uncle. Who lay on my bed with his shirt rucked up to his neck and told me to take him, who said he wanted to lick our shared come off me and suck me until I was hard again.

Vin, who went from strong and confident to soft and almost vulnerable, who looked so goddamn good in a gold chain I hurt, who was turning into the very definition of what I was looking for in a lover.

I slumped back in my chair, stunned and more than a little scared.

Josh clapped me reassuringly on the shoulder and rose. "I'll get you another espresso, double shot," he said, and went back up to the counter.

Chapter Nineteen

Every Fierro learned how to handle going to church past confirmation.

Initially they all fell for the well-laid trap of being told, now that they were adults in the eyes of God and fully initiated into the Church, they could decide when they attended. Sometimes a well-meaning elder cousin or sibling would warn them not to stop going altogether and would try to give tips, but nearly universally every one of them seized on the moment of freedom and started partying late on Saturday night and hanging out to watch TV in their bedrooms well past noon mass. The golden period never lasted more than the first month and a half, at which point one of the Fathers would pay a visit to the new adult's mother and inform her of the lack of attendance. Depending on the mood of the parents, a harsh lecture or serving of guilt with more layers than Marco's lasagna always followed.

Church didn't have to happen every week, but it still had to happen. For his part, Vince went about every third weekend, which was slightly more than absolutely necessary but less than was ideal, and usually his mother would cluck her tongue and shake her head when the subject came up. He was never sure if the bigger problem was that he went when most of the family didn't go or when *she* didn't go.

This Sunday was a Fierro command performance, however, because at ten o'clock mass, Vince's second cousin once removed would be baptized. The entire family was present. As Vince gravitated to his usual seat at these occasions next to

Rachel in his family's pew, he saw the prodigals returning with their standard reluctance to the fold: Adamo, Rina, Cessy, Patrick and Hank.

Vince couldn't help watching Hank as he made his way into the pew on the other side of the aisle. Hank was ten years older than Vince, but he seemed more like twenty. His hair was thin on the top of his head, as thin as the rest of him. The women always worried over Hank with no one to cook for him. Vince had to admit, his cousin did look a little sickly. Was that because he was sick? Was it because he was that uneasy about being here?

"Quit staring," Rachel hissed at him, and Vince averted his eyes.

Mass slid over him like a comfortable blanket, and he rose and knelt and murmured along at the appropriate moments in the haze he'd perfected in fourth grade. His thoughts kept returning to Hank, however. He'd come alone. Was he alone? Did he have someone he wished he could bring, or was he single?

He wondered if he should have invited Trey.

They'd seen each other a lot lately, as much as possible with Trey's school and work schedule. He knew the people at Full Moon had figured out he and Trey were seeing each other. He was pretty sure he liked them knowing too.

They were dating. Seeing each other. Trey wasn't pushing him to make it public, but it was getting close to time. By this point in any relationship with a girl, he would have at least taken her to dinner at one of the restaurants. He'd have invited him to this event today.

What did it say about him that he hadn't considered it? Did this make him smart, or an ass?

The baptism was the same as any other, another baby in a white dress, another pair of beaming parents, another set of cousins standing at attention as sponsors. Vince had done it himself three times and didn't have to be prompted for his responses during the ceremony anymore. He did, though, feel the usual pang of regret for never having gone up for the other set of responses, and today the idea of possibly getting serious with Trey, of thinking of bringing him to family events, of maybe, potentially, considering him family—well, playing parents at a baptism would be out, wouldn't it.

Of course, they could adopt.

The gravity of this kind of thinking shook him hard enough to make him stumble over a refrain, and his head couldn't hold much more than white noise for the rest of the ceremony. He walked with Rachel from the church to the restaurant in disquiet.

"Talk to him," Rachel said eventually.

Vince blinked at her, confused. "Who?"

Rachel rolled her eyes. "The Pope. *Hank.* I can see your mind working from here. And I saw you staring at him. If you want to know what it's like being gay in the Fierro family, take him outside for a smoke and talk to him."

That wasn't what he'd been thinking about, not exactly, but Vince nodded. She left him alone after that for the rest of the walk, and once they got to the restaurant, Aunt Eva pulled her aside to tell her about the handsome young man who'd come into her sister's shop, and Vince ended up wandering near his father and Marco.

He didn't talk to Hank, but he watched him. Watched him linger at the fringes, watched him take a seat alone. He saw the others steer clear of Hank as well, glancing at him, exchanging painful, awkward waves. It was almost as if he had a force field around him.

It upset Vince. It wasn't right. Hank was family. Someone should sit with him.

He decided he would be the one to do it.

He'd finish this scotch, though, to bolster his courage.

Two scotches later, dinner was about to be served, and Vince was pretty sure he was ready to commandeer a seat next to his cousin. He maneuvered his way through a sea of children, around a group of teenagers and past a group of aunts who were whispering intently near the bar. They kept glancing at Hank, and since Vince wasn't moving as swiftly as usual with a few drinks in him, he couldn't help overhearing what his Aunt Fina was saying.

"—heard he was with a boy. An *escort*, someone he hired for sex. Except it was a sting, and he got *arrested*. Alberto had to bail him out of jail."

Vince slowed way, way down, acting like he was looking across the room for someone, training his ears like sonar.

"Can you imagine? A *grown man* doing such a thing." Fina clucked her tongue.

"That's how they are. The gay lifestyle. That's all it is." Vince couldn't see his cousin's wife Olivia, but he could hear the pinched outrage in her voice. "He shouldn't even be allowed in here."

"He's family," someone else said.

"People like that aren't family. Not the kind of family I want around."

Vince cleared his throat and stumbled back the way he'd come. His mother came around the corner from the kitchen, smiling at him. "They're about to serve, hon. Why don't you take a seat by your father and I?"

"I just gotta hit the restrooms quick," he told her, nodding in their direction.

"Sure." She patted him on the shoulder with a wink. "Fair warning—I heard a rumor you're seeing someone again. I won't let you leave the table until I've heard all about her."

Vince's insides churned. "Really gotta go, Mom."

She kissed him on the cheek. "I'll be waiting."

He didn't go to the restroom. He went outside, where an

April rain had started, and stood underneath the awning, hands shaking as he lit a cigarette from the secret stash he and some of the cousins kept behind the loose shutter for emergencies. He smoked four of them.

People like that aren't family.

Tucking the cigarettes into his shirt pocket, Vince turned up his collar and headed out into the rain.

Chapter Twenty

Just when I'd started to think everything between us was good, that maybe I loved Vincent Fierro, that maybe I could introduce him to my friends and maybe even kiss my virginity goodbye, he got weird on me.

First, he didn't show up at the coffee shop like he always did. I texted him, but got no answer. I thought for sure he'd be waiting for me when I got home, but he wasn't.

"Hey, Gram, did Vinnie call?"

"Not today, honey."

Still, I didn't think much of it. He had a job. He had family. He was probably busy. But when the second day passed with still no word, and then the third, I became worried. A little seed of doubt began to grow.

I texted him several times on the fourth day. On the fifth day I called. He didn't answer. I left a voicemail, but he didn't call back.

On the sixth day, I was angry. I spent a lot of time composing long diatribes in my head where I told him that the least he could do was offer me an explanation.

On the seventh day, I fought back tears.

On the eighth day, my phone rang. A glance at the screen told me it was him.

Not sure if this would be an apology or a kiss-off and feeling vulnerable because Tara was starting to get pushy about meeting the man who was possibly about to dump me for reasons I didn't understand, I answered cautiously. "Hello?"

"Trey!" Wherever he was, it was loud. I could hear music in the background, and people laughing. He was practically shouting. "What are you doing tonight?"

"Writing a paper."

"*What*? I can't hear you!"

"Writing a paper!" I said, louder this time. At least Gram would have her hearing aid out by now. I didn't have to worry about disturbing her. "Where are you?"

"I'm at Mr. Joe's."

"What are you doing all the way over there?" Mr. Joe's was a bar close to my house, and close to his family's restaurant, but I knew it wasn't a place he normally went.

"I wanted a drink."

"Sounds like you've had a few already." More than a few, if his slurred words were any indication.

"Yeah, maybe," he said, sounding amused. "So what? You should come have a drink with me."

I glanced at my watch. Only nine o'clock, and yet I still had a paper to finish, and though I didn't work the next morning, I had to be up at five if I hoped to beat the crowd at the computer lab so I could type it up. "Not tonight, Vin."

"Come on, Trey. You work too hard."

"I haven't heard from you all week."

"I know, but you're hearing from me now. Come down here and let me buy you a beer."

"Vinnie, has it occurred to you that I hardly ever drink?"

"Yeah, but..." His words died out. No, it hadn't occurred to him at all.

"I have to go."

"No, Trey, don't hang up. Just one beer, okay? What would it hurt?"

I was surprised by what I heard in his voice. Disappointment. Maybe even a hint of desperation. "Why?" I asked.

"Because. That's all." That was all he said, but I could hear it in his voice—it was the defensive tone he always used when I pushed too close. The same tone he used when he said, "I'm not gay."

I bit back my urge to laugh. I bit back my urge to cry. I thought about the fact that he'd obviously come over to the neighborhood to see me. He'd probably run out of nerve and stopped at the bar on his way. Even if he had to be drunk to do it, he had actually called. Finally.

I pondered the ways this could go: me giving in, or not. Him saying what was really on his mind.

Or not.

"Vinnie," I said at last. "Repeat after me: 'I've missed you, Trey.'"

"Fuck, Trey, it's just a beer."

"Okay. If you say so. I have to finish my paper now, but—"

"Goddamn it!"

"—maybe we can get together on Saturday—"

"All right." He sighed heavily. "Just a minute. Let me at least go outside where I can fucking hear you."

What he meant was, let him go outside where nobody would hear *him*, but I didn't push it.

The noise of the bar died, and I imagined him pushing through the dirty glass door of the old building. I pictured him hunching against the brick wall of Mr. Joe's, his arms crossed over his chest. I could practically sense him glancing around to make sure nobody was near enough to hear. "Fine," he said at last. "I've missed you."

Not exactly sincere. More grudging than accepting, but it was a start.

"Good. Now say, 'Please come have a drink with me, Trey.'"

He sighed again, but it sounded a bit like laughter. When

he spoke, I thought he might even have been smiling. "Please come have a drink with me, Trey." And then, without me coaching him at all, he added, "*Please. I'd really like to see you.*"

He wanted to see me.

I was such a fool. I was so crazy about him that his confession made me feel like I could fly. I bit my lip, smiling and hoping he couldn't somehow tell. I closed my eyes and let the simple joy of that statement fill me up for just a minute.

When I opened them again, reality set in—reality in the form of a mostly blank piece of paper in front of me, an open textbook and my notes a fucking mess around me. If only I could afford a computer, then I wouldn't have to get up so early to go type it up. Of course, that still wouldn't solve the issue of having to write the thing. Going out tonight was a bad idea any way I looked at it.

"Please," Vinnie said, and for better or worse, this time, he really did sound sincere. "Let me see you tonight."

A lifetime of being responsible, of never missing a due date, of always being on time, and it boiled down to this: Hadn't I earned the right to cut myself some slack? Would it be so bad, just this once, to be one of the schmucks who turned in their paper a day late?

The age-old dilemma of responsibility versus desire warred inside my head, and it took very little for me to choose the victor.

"I'll be there in twenty minutes."

I found him sitting at the bar, and he'd somehow managed to secure the stool next to him for me. I sat down, looking over into his dark eyes. Under cover of the bar, his hand found mine, and he squeezed my fingers. "Thanks for coming."

Something was wrong, I realized, and it wasn't anything to do with me. Something had upset him. I wanted to find out what it was, but I had no idea how to ask. Nobody had to tell me the direct approach would get me nowhere.

What if he was going to break up with me? What if he couldn't bear to do it over the phone, so he'd called me here? What if he was just working up the courage?

What if I'd fallen in love with him like Josh had said, and he was about to let me go?

"Can I buy you a drink?" He squeezed my hand again. "You want a Sprite, or water?"

I debated my options. I rarely drank, but not for the reasons most people assumed. It wasn't because I hated alcohol. It wasn't that I felt I could get back at it for what it had done to my mom by pretending it didn't exist. After all, despite what my mom claimed, alcohol hadn't done anything to her. She'd done all the damage on her own. The thing was, alcohol simply wasn't convenient. It cost money, and more importantly, it cost time. Between two jobs and school, I didn't have the luxury of dealing with hangovers.

But tonight? Well, I'd already decided to throw responsibility to the wind.

"How about a screwdriver?"

Vince's eyes widened a little, but he said nothing, only flagged down the bartender and ordered my drink.

Two hours later, I'd finished two screwdrivers, and I could feel them starting to work. I was slowly nursing my way through a third. Vinnie, on the other hand, had finished several drinks, and if he was going to break up with me, he had a damn funny way of going about it. The normally uptight, I'm Not Gay man I'd come to know was turning into somebody else entirely. He kept touching me and leaning too close. He even kissed me, first my jaw and then my ear, and then a slow, lingering kiss on my lips that made me want to melt.

This new Vinnie didn't seem to care that we were in a bar in a neighborhood where he might be recognized. He put one arm around my shoulder and pulled me halfway off my stool.

"I really have missed you," he whispered in my ear. "I

couldn't stop thinking about you."

I'd missed him too, more than I could say, but I was still hurt enough not to want to admit it. "I was beginning to think we were over."

"I was being stupid, I know. Tell me I'm forgiven."

Not exactly an apology, but it made my heart swell just the same. "You might be."

He chuckled. "Fair enough." He nipped at my ear, raising goose bumps down my spine. "Come home with me."

"That's a bad idea." But the truth was, the thought made my heart race.

"Please." His warm breath tickled my neck. His other hand was sliding slowly up my leg. "God, I want to be able to touch you."

"Vin—"

"I know the rule. No sex. I know." He cupped my groin in his hand, and my eyes drifted shut. I bit my cheek to stifle the whimper threatening to escape my lips. "I'm not asking you to break the rules," he whispered. "But I'd sure love to explore that line between yes and no."

It was such a bad, bad idea. It could only lead to trouble. It could only lead to regrets.

"Please," he said again.

I finished my drink before we left, even though my head was already spinning. It was cold outside. The mist in the air was trying to coalesce into rain. Soon, it would succeed. I shoved my hands deep into my pockets and followed him down the street to the station.

Bad idea. Bad idea. Bad idea.

The words were like a mantra in my head, echoing with every step.

Bad idea.

We waited for the train. Not speaking. Not touching. Not

daring to look at each other.

I should say no. I should turn around and go home.

There was still time, until the train pulled up and the doors swished open and I was following him inside.

Bad idea.

Onto the train, which was almost deserted. Sitting side by side, his hand on my knee.

Bad idea. Really bad idea.

Five stops. People got on. People got off. My mouth was dry. My heart was pounding.

Bad idea.

Thoughts were flying through my head at such a frantic pace, I began to feel sick.

For so long, I'd been hanging on to my virginity as if it was some kind of prize to be given away. It wasn't because I thought sex was a sin. It wasn't that I thought we had to be married. It was simply that I wanted it to matter. I wanted it to be with somebody who I thought was worth the risk of opening myself up.

Right now, though, I wanted it to be Vinnie.

Whether or not he loved me the way I did him wasn't the point. It didn't matter that it might not last. It only mattered that right now, I cared about him, and if I slept with him, it would mean something to us both.

Still, I didn't know if I was ready. So what was I doing on the train with him?

Bad idea.

Lights seemed to fly past the window, and Vinnie's hand moved farther up my thigh.

I'll get off at the next stop, I thought. *I'll just hop on the train going the other way. I'll say good night. I'll tell him about my paper, and about having to be up early. I'll tell him this is a bad idea.*

Then suddenly we were alone on the train. He pulled me close. He kissed my neck. His hand moved slowly to my groin. His lips were warm and his breath tickled my ear. My pants felt way too tight over my erection, and still the words were in my head.

Bad, bad fucking idea.

I missed the next station and any that might have come after. I was lost in the warm glow of my buzz and the frantic thoughts inside my mind. His kisses and the gentle insistence of his touch were the only things anchoring me to the world. The train stopped, and then he was leading me off, holding my hand, guiding me through the damp, cold night down a street I didn't recognize, up stairs I didn't know. He let go of me to unlock the door.

Oh God, this is such a bad idea.

And then we were inside. He grabbed me. He pulled me into his arms and kissed me, and God, it felt good. He was so solid and strong. And so *sure.* For once, there was no hesitation. He led me through the room, down a hallway, kissing me the whole way. He smelled amazing, like he always did, and the sour taste of beer mixed with the heat of his mouth seemed like perfection. Somehow my shirt was off, and so was his, and his skin against mine was smooth and warm and intoxicating.

He pushed me down onto the bed, and somewhere, way in the back of my mind, an alarm went off. An echo of my mantra—*bad idea*—but it was only for a moment. The room was dark. He was heavy on top of me, his groin grinding into me. My hands were still cold from being outside, and the skin of his back felt feverish. The furnace hummed. The first drops of rain pattered on the window. The only other sound was us—our frantic breathing and desperate moans.

With the warmth of the vodka in my veins, the weight of him on top of me, the gentle racket of the rain hitting the window, it was so easy to let go. It was so easy to hush that voice and the alarm in my head. His hands were everywhere, his kisses becoming more urgent.

"God, Trey, I've missed you so much. You're all I've thought about for days."

He rolled us over so I was on top. He wrapped his legs around my hips. That alarm again, in the back of my mind, and I hushed it. I didn't want to heed it. I just wanted to touch him and to finally let our desire for each other reach its logical conclusion.

Vinnie kissed behind my ear. "Spend the night with me."

"Shhh," I told him, turning my head to claim his lips. I didn't want him to talk. I didn't want him to wake the voice of reason that always ruled my head. For once, I wanted to be impulsive and irrational and reckless. For once, I wanted to let myself give in.

His legs tightened around me. "You turn me on so much."

The alarm continued, and I hated it. I ignored it. I ran my hand down his stomach to his pants, which had somehow come unbuttoned. Had I done that? I slid my hand inside, rubbing him through the fabric of his briefs, and he moaned.

"Yes," he hissed. "Lower."

I obliged him, moving my hand down to cup his scrotum. He bucked against me, and I strained to fight back my own arousal. Did he have condoms? I knew I should ask, but I couldn't come up with the bravery needed to say the words. If I spoke, the spell would be broken. Reason would rear its ugly head.

"Lower," he whispered. He arched toward me, lifting his hips, so my hand slid down between his legs.

The way he responded to my touch amazed me. He pulled me down and kissed me hungrily, grinding his ass toward my exploring fingers. Even through the thin fabric of his briefs, I knew when I'd found his entrance. The timbre of his moan changed. My hand was between my groin and his ass, and I shoved my hips forward, letting my motion and my questing fingers simulate the feeling of thrusting into him.

"Is this what you want?" I asked.

He opened his eyes, although in the dark I couldn't read what was in them. "Yes." He strained back against my fingers. "I want you in me. I want all of you in me."

His answer shocked me. It scared me. It also turned me on beyond belief. It had never occurred to me that he'd want to bottom. I'd always assumed he'd want to top, and my own fear of being penetrated for the first time had worked in my favor, helping to temper whatever arousal I might feel. But now, here he was, pushing down onto my hand, letting my fingers slide deeper, moaning as he did.

"Please, Trey," he whispered. "God, I want you."

The alarm was sounding again in my brain, and I wanted to ignore it. I didn't want to hear it at all, let alone heed it. I wanted to rush forward, to let this be the night when I learned what it felt like to be with another man. But there was something so wrong about what was happening.

"I don't think we should." I only said it because I thought I should. Not because I meant it.

"Please, Trey." His hands began to fumble at the buttons on my jeans. "I want you to fuck me. God, I want you to fuck me so much."

His words and the unapologetic desperation of his tone made the alarm blare.

I want you to fuck me. The words seemed to resound in my head. And they were all wrong.

This was Vinnie, the man who couldn't say he was gay. He couldn't tell me he missed me. He could barely even tell me he wanted to see me without me coaxing him through it. And now, here he was, his legs wrapped around my hips, his ass grinding against my hand, my fingers and the fabric of his briefs inside him up to my first knuckle, and he was begging me to fuck him.

The glow of arousal began to fade. I removed my hands out

of his pants. I backed away a bit, trying to catch my breath.

"Trey, please," he said again. "God, *please.*"

I pushed his hands away from the buttons on my pants, and I made myself think. I made myself notice the slur of his words, the clumsiness of his hands. I thought about how much he'd had to drink. And at last, responsibility won out, as it always seemed to do for me.

Vinnie may have wanted me to fuck him, but I knew that had he been sober, he would never have been able to admit it, let alone beg for it. Chances were he couldn't even admit it to himself in the cool, clear light of day. I was pretty sure if I gave him what he was asking for, he'd hate me for it in the end. He'd wake up in the morning and not be able to look me in the eye. Whatever we had between us would be over before it started, and I'd have exchanged my years of waiting for nothing but regrets. Yes, Vincent Fierro was probably going to be the guy I lost my virginity to, but it wasn't going to be tonight.

I took a deep breath, and although it felt like killing some tiny piece of me, I said, "Remember our rules, Vin. No sex."

"No!" he moaned, reaching again for my pants. "Trey, come on."

"No."

"You can't stop now. You know you want this as much as I do."

"I do, Vinnie. But not like this."

"Don't be a tease."

If I'd had any doubt that it was the alcohol talking instead of him, that statement dispelled them. He'd always respected my limits before, and even though I'd followed him to his apartment on the pretense of exploring that boundary, I knew the real Vinnie, the *sober* Vinnie, would never have said that word to me.

"Okay," I said, untangling myself from his limbs. "You get undressed and get into bed."

He practically knocked me off the bed onto the floor in his haste to obey. In the faint light from the window, I watched him shed his pants. I turned away when he bent to remove his briefs. When I turned back around, he was in bed, the covers pulled up far enough to make a tent over his erection. I was glad I couldn't see the look in his eyes.

"What about you?" he asked.

"Give me a minute to get ready."

What that meant, I had no idea, and I was glad he was too drunk to ask. I went into the bathroom. I put the lid down on the toilet and sat on it with my head in my hands. I took deep breaths until my heart had stopped pounding and my hands no longer shook. I waited until my erection was gone. I found some kind of martyr-like comfort in the dull ache that resided in my scrotum, reminding me that I'd forgone the release I so desperately needed.

By the time I emerged, Vinnie was snoring softly, sound asleep, exactly as I'd planned. The rain outside pelted the window, now a heavy staccato instead of a light patter. The thought of going out into that cold, miserable weather and riding the train home alone made my heart sink. I checked the clock. It was after midnight. I was tired. Even if I left now, I still wouldn't finish my paper. I wasn't even sure I'd bother going to class the next day.

Here in Vinnie's bedroom, it was warm and comforting. His bed looked like heaven.

"Vinnie?" I asked, unsure if I wanted him to wake or not. I wanted to ask if I could stay, but I didn't want to risk him remembering where we'd left off.

It didn't matter. He was out cold.

I stripped down to my boxers and climbed into the empty side of the bed. It was a long time though before I fell asleep.

Chapter Twenty-One

When Vince woke up the next morning, he felt like seven kinds of hell. Groaning, he tried to roll over, hoping he could make it to the toilet before he threw up.

That was when he heard the toilet flush. Somebody was in his apartment.

In his *bathroom.*

A different kind of sick swamped him, and he frantically tried to recall the night before, worried he'd picked up some whore at a bar and taken her home, ready to beat himself into next week for being such an idiot, wondering if Trey would ever forgive him.

The bathroom door opened, and Vince made himself look, ready to try to tell whatever woman came out of it that he'd made a terrible, horrible mistake—

But it wasn't a woman who walked out of the bathroom. It was Trey, wearing nothing but his boxers, appearing tired and frazzled, but still as sexy as hell.

A wave of relief washed over Vince, but it didn't last long. What exactly had he done?

"I used your toothbrush," Trey said, not quite meeting his eyes as he crawled back into bed. "I'm sorry. I know that's gross, but I was desperate."

After everything that had happened, Trey was worried about using his toothbrush? Carefully, so carefully, Vince turned over to lie on his side so he could face Trey.

I'm a bastard. The lowest, scum-sucking bastard that ever

lived. He ignored the pounding in his head and touched Trey's face, ready to do any penance he was asked. "I'm so sorry," he croaked.

Trey lifted an eyebrow at him, then smiled a sad little smile before politely moving his hand away. "You're forgiven."

Oh, no. Vince knew penance, and this wasn't it.

"I've been such an ass this past week, not even returning your calls. I just..." He wanted to explain it, but he wasn't sure he could. Not yet. "I wanted to see you, but I was so scared."

"Of what?"

A valid question, and one he deserved an answer to, but first Vince wanted to know how much of a jerk he'd been the night before. "I can't remember much of last night, but I don't have any doubt I was a drunken, idiot ass." His stomach lurched. "Did I...? Did we...?"

Now Trey looked mildly pissed. "You honestly think I'd let my first time be with someone so drunk he can't stand up?"

Vince started to stammer an apology, then went very still as he realized what Trey had said. He'd thought he'd imagined it, but then Trey moved his gaze away.

Vince moved up—carefully—to rest on his elbow as he stared down at Trey in disbelief. "Are you telling me...? Are you saying that you...?"

"I told you." Trey's cheeks were pink. "I don't date."

"Yeah, but I thought you meant you didn't date anymore. I didn't know you'd never...dated."

His cheeks turned pinker. "Is that a problem?"

Fuck yes, it was a problem. Vince remembered enough of the night before to know he'd been pressuring Trey to go to bed with him, and the idea that he'd been doing that to a virgin— *drunk*—made him feel lower than the belly of a snake. "Why didn't you tell me?"

"Because I didn't want you looking at me like I was a freak. Like you are right now."

Vince scowled. "I don't think you're a freak. I think I'm an ass."

"You are. But you're a sexy ass."

Vince couldn't share the joke. "I should have figured it out. That's just like you, to wait for something special, and there I was so wrapped up in my own problems I ignored you and what you needed." *Like everyone else in your life.*

Trey rolled his eyes, but Vince could tell his words were appreciated. *Good.*

"I know I was pressuring you, and I'm sorry. I really am."

This time, Trey smiled. "It's okay."

"It won't happen again. I promise."

He was surprised at the way those words made Trey's smile disappear. "I don't want your promise."

"What?"

Trey sighed. "Never mind. You're forgiven." He turned toward Vince, reaching out to stroke his bare arm. "But I want you to talk to me. I know something's wrong. There must be a reason you've been avoiding me."

Ass, ass, ass. That's what I am, first-class asshole. "I'm sorry." How many times would he have to say it before he felt better? "I didn't mean to ignore you. I... Something happened Sunday, and it's really upset me. I should have talked to you about it, but..."

Trey scooted over and kissed his forearm. "Talk to me about it now."

Vince didn't want to talk about it. His head was pounding, his gut felt like it had knives in it, and that was just from thinking about repeating what he'd heard his family saying, not what the overindulgence of alcohol was doing to him. But Trey deserved an explanation.

He didn't know how he could say it without falling apart.

Trey's fingers stroked Vince's chest, teasing the whorls of

hair leading to his briefs. It was a comforting touch, intimate, and oddly soothing to the part of him so afraid to speak the truth. It stirred things deep within Vince, things he'd never told anyone at all, not even Rachel. That simple touch was a flood loose inside him. Vince thought he might be ready to let it out.

Shutting his eyes, shaking a little, he settled back down onto his pillow, clutching at Trey's hand as he began to speak.

He told him everything.

"I was twelve when I realized what I felt for some of my guy friends was different, that it was wrong. I'd called everybody fag like the rest of the kids, but I didn't get it until then, what it meant. I knew it was a sin, that it would make everyone mad at me, that it would make me different and shut me out. So I shut it out instead. I did what I was supposed to do, believing it would make everything okay. I dated girls, I scolded myself when I noticed guys. I screwed around a little in college, with one guy in particular, but never very far, and not for long. I told myself it was bad, that I could say no, that I should say no. Every time it crept up on me, I ran. I never let myself look back.

"I married my first wife because she got knocked up. I might not have been the father, but she told me I was, and she was a good girl, and my mama cried, so I married her. She miscarried." He swallowed hard, remembering that pain, of gearing up to be a father and then finding out he wouldn't be. "I helped her through that. Helped her through school too. Helped her family when they needed things. I fucking helped her in and out of cars. I took out the trash and did the odd jobs around the house and didn't press her to make love when she had a headache." He shut his eyes, embarrassed at the rest. "She left after eighteen months and married some friend of her sister's eight months later. They have four kids now."

Trey kissed his shoulder. Vince turned away from Trey's face so he wouldn't have to see any pity and continued.

"Patty, my second wife, didn't want to have sex until marriage. So we didn't, and when it felt right, I asked her to marry me. I thought this time would be fine. Same thing: did what I thought I was supposed to. Took her out to nice dinners. She liked seeing shows. I took her to the shows." His jaw set and he shook his head. "She didn't even last a year. Said I wasn't involved. Said she didn't feel like she knew me. I told her if she wasn't happy, I wouldn't stand in her way if she wanted to go. She left." The story was starting to get to him, so he sped it up. "Amelia was the same, except I sort of think I know what I did. I bothered her too much, asking if she was happy. She said I tried too *hard*. And she left too.

"So I stopped. Stopped dating. Slept around a little for awhile, but then I just stopped. Then there was this long dry spell, and then there was that call to the gay couple in Lakeview." He realized he hadn't ever told Trey about that, so he filled out the rest. "They had a broken disposal, but they were so sweet and so happy, even when they were upset, and I ached just looking at them. I wanted that. And for the first time ever, I let myself admit I wanted it with a man." He shivered at the terror of that admission. "I tried to walk away from it, but I couldn't shake it. I went down to the restaurant, thinking that would square me up, being with my family, reminding me what I'd lose, and I saw you with your group project and thought you were cute."

Trey's soft laugh caressed his soul. "You did not," he said in a voice that made it clear he wanted to believe Vince did.

"I did so, and it freaked me the fuck out, so I went to talk to Rachel. I told her what I was feeling, scared to death of what would happen when I said it out loud, trying like hell to say I wasn't gay, but she's Rach, so of course she didn't bat an eye and yelled at me for saying gay men were effeminate. Which I don't think I did, but it didn't matter, she still wanted to kick my ass. She told me to go to a gay bar and see what happened, to try and sort myself out. I went, and it was awful, and I was just about ready to leave and call it a bust when you came up to me."

Trey found his hand and laced their fingers together, and Vince squeezed back.

"The rest you know, except there's this cousin of mine. He's the one they warn you about when you don't get married and have babies in time. You don't want to be like Hank, they say. Lonely old Hank up in the burbs. Hank is the horrible warning, and we all nod and say of course we don't want to be like Hank. Except I found out from Rachel that Hank is gay, that this is why he stays away. I thought maybe it was just a misunderstanding, or that maybe somehow if I fixed things for Hank, it would be okay for me." He swallowed hard. "Sunday I found out there wasn't any chance of that. I heard my aunts and cousins talking about Hank, about him being gay, and they said...they said people like that aren't family."

The words caught at rough edges in his throat. For a moment the confession hung there, terrible and weighty, the monster ready to consume him raw and whole.

Trey shifted closer, put his arms around Vince's chest and kissed his shoulder, keeping the beast at bay.

Vince turned his face into Trey's hair as he closed his eyes. "I'm gay," he whispered. "I always have been. I tried to run from it, and it was like I ran from my life. I thought I was a fuckup, that there was something wrong with me that kept me from being happy. Except with you I am happy, and it's not just because you're sweet and strong and sexy and amazing." He squeezed Trey close, more to steady himself than anything else. "It's because for the first time I'm actually being myself. I feel like a kid when I'm with you, and it's not because I'm a dirty old man. It's because I think I am a kid when I'm with you, the twelve-year-old who got scared and packed himself away because he thought he was a sin. And maybe I am. Except it doesn't feel like one, not even close." He let out a shaky breath. "I want to have a relationship with a man. With you. I really, really don't want to screw up anymore." His heart broke, and tears he didn't realize he'd been holding back leaked silently out of the sides of his eyes. "But I don't want to lose my family."

For a long time they lay there, holding each other, Vince trembling as he wept silently, reverberating from everything he'd laid out, not just to Trey but to himself. *I'm gay,* he repeated, tasting the words, getting used to the panic they set loose inside him. *I'm gay. I'm gay, and it's all right. I'm gay, and my family won't like it, and I don't know how to tell them, and I might lose them all forever, but it's still okay. Somehow, it's all going to be okay.*

Trey pressed a soft kiss in the center of Vince's bare chest. Then he said, very quietly, "I love you."

Vince didn't move.

"I love you." Trey lifted his head and looked Vince in the eye, touching his face, his blue eyes radiating calm and peace and...well, love. "I don't want to make you lose your family. I wouldn't blame you if you chose them over me, and I'll understand if you have to. But I do love you. And I know it sounds like a bad line, but I think I always will, at least a little." His fingers traced a circle over Vince's heart. "No matter what happens."

Vince could barely breathe. His head was a riot of thought, of memory, of those sharp, terrible moments when he'd known, when he'd pushed away, when he'd been so sure that if he ever let that part of him out, the world would end. Those old ghosts rose up, trying to scare him back into place, but Trey's words cut them down one by one.

Maybe, they whispered. *Maybe, just maybe, you can be you and not have to be alone.*

Vince let the terrifying hopes take root, sure they would die off, but they only became stronger. So strong that eventually he couldn't take it anymore. With a relief he hadn't even hoped to know sliding over him, he bent down, rested his forehead on his lover's chest and cried like a little boy who had found his way home.

Trey put his arms around Vince, kissed his hair and promised over and over again that everything would be okay.

Chapter Twenty-Two

I don't know why I was so nervous for the guys to meet Vin, but I was.

I guess it was because they didn't know him like I did, or Gram, and they were the first people I cared about who might not like him or understand him. I feared they'd think he was too old, too closeted, too Italian or too something else I hadn't thought of yet. While I knew their reservations would come from wanting to protect me, the meeting Tara had insisted on having still had my stomach in knots.

Weirdly, Vinnie himself seemed fine about it. Not only that, but he took it seriously. I could tell, because he dressed up—but not too much—and left the gold chain at home. When we went into the coffee shop Tara had picked, Vinnie stood straight and tall, deferring to me to make introductions but playing older man next door to the nines as soon as I'd presented him. It wasn't until he held out my chair for me to sit down that I realized why he was so comfortable: Vin had met the family before. A lot.

I was his first gay family, though, which made me feel special.

Still, it didn't matter how smooth he played it to Tara. She gave him the tenth degree.

"So you're not out," she said, leaning forward to regard him cynically over her steaming latte. I tried to kick her under the table, but she moved her feet out of the way and kept her focus on Vin.

Vin, to his credit, nodded, looking only a little stiff. "Not yet. This is all sort of new to me."

"I hear it's different for your generation," Dillon said, more of a dig at Vin's age than an expression of empathy. He, unfortunately, was too far away to kick.

I came to Vin's rescue instead. "He comes from a huge Catholic family too, and they've made it clear it isn't cool to be gay. Besides, Vin hasn't been out to himself very long."

He gave me a look that was part amusement, part *I got this.* "I'm going to come out, even to them. It's just a matter of figuring out how best to do it."

Josh was dubious. "How can you be as old as you are and not know you're gay?"

"He's not *old*," I shot back.

Dillon spoke before Vin could. "Well, it's not as simple for everyone as you're trying to make it out to be," he said to Josh. "That Catholic shit can be brutal. Haven't you heard that bullshit the Pope has been spouting lately, all those edicts to crack down on the evil gay?"

"My church isn't that bad," Vin interjected. "Though honestly, I go as little as I can get away with. I don't care what the Pope thinks, though. I care what my family thinks. I want to believe they'll come around when it's gay Vinnie they're dealing with, not some abstract bastard up in Boystown, but I can't say for sure that's what will happen." He shrugged with more nonchalance than I knew he felt. "It will be what it will be."

"But you are coming out?" Tara pressed. "For Trey?"

"God, you guys, lay the fuck off," I said, unable to take any more.

Vinnie put his hand over mine under the table, but he didn't look away from Tara. "No, not for Trey. For me."

Dillon leaned back in his chair, nodding in approval. "Good."

I rolled my eyes at the idea of Dillon being Gay Guru, but

somehow this closed the grilling and let us move on to other topics.

"You're all in school?" Vinnie asked.

"I'm in grad school," Tara supplied, "but the guys are out. Dillon works at Logan Enterprises downtown."

"I push paper around," Dillon clarified with a wry grin.

He did more than that, but Josh spoke before I could. "I work at the Southside Society. A homeless shelter," he added, a bit of challenge in his voice. Josh was a pretty big bleeding heart. "And you're a plumber, right?"

Vince nodded, unashamed. "At the moment. I've done a little bit of everything."

"He's an MBA," I supplied, not without pride. But this only made them wrinkle their noses.

"Why are you a plumber if you have an MBA?" Dillon asked.

Vinnie shrugged, but there was a twinkle in his eye. "You got something against plumbing?"

Dillon faltered. "Well, no, but—"

"Get the plumbing in something wrong, and you'll be sorry fast. Plus, plumbing never gets boring. Dirty and gross, yes, but never boring."

Josh smiled. "But numbers do?"

Vinnie nodded at him, smiling back. "They do."

The whole thing went pretty smoothly after that. While Vin didn't exactly slide into our groove, he played along well, and actually I was pretty proud of him, how he handled what had been at times open hostility. When we finally wandered back to the EL to head home, I felt upbeat, and I grabbed his hand and cuddled openly against his arm.

We were still close to Little Italy, and usually unless it was dark we were pretty circumspect about touching this close to people who might recognize Vinnie. He didn't shove me away, but he did tense up just a little, and I started to back off, not wanting to push him when he'd already done so much for me. To my surprise though, he didn't let me go. Instead, he pulled me closer and brushed a kiss against my hair.

"You don't have to," I said quietly, though I was loving every second of it.

"Maybe I want to."

"Are you really going to come out? To your family and everything?" I asked as we turned onto Loomis.

"It's either that or live two lives, and I don't want to do that."

"What if they don't accept you?"

He shrugged. "Then I try to change their mind. Or mourn them and find my own way."

It was such a far cry from his despair of the week before, but it fit with his demeanor at lunch and a calmness I'd felt in him lately in general. We didn't say anything more, but he kept me close all the way to my front door, where he gave me a long, sensual kiss on my front steps before waving me inside.

I lingered, wanting to invite him in, wanting to take him directly up to my room and continue the kind of exploring we'd done that one day when I'd been so angry, the things he'd begged me to do to him when he was drunk. I'd thought about sex with Vin a lot. I'd admitted I loved him. I'd decided he was going to be my first. Yet something in me kept holding back, dragging the moment out. I was starting to think it might be fear, though what I was afraid of I couldn't figure out. I wanted Vin, and he wanted me. I wanted sex period. Everything was lined up and ready. What was I waiting for?

I let him go, smiling at him as I watched him disappear up the street. Then I went inside and closed the door.

Mom was passed out on the sofa.

Not just sleeping. *Passed out.* Drunk and high, drool congealing in the corner of her mouth before it dripped onto the cushion. Her hair was unkempt and greasy, and her housecoat was stained, sagging open at her neck to reveal the pasty, unhealthy flesh above her breasts. She snored softly, but even this sound seemed off, not right.

In her hand was an empty brown medicine bottle, and the stench of sweat and sticky-sweet-raspberry flavoring hung in the air.

I turned away and headed up the stairs, shutting my door with angry force, though I knew it wouldn't wake her. I paced around my room a few minutes, telling myself I was getting rid of my anger before I settled down to work, but I kept smelling that smell stuck in my nose, kept seeing her lying there.

They'd warned her about the cough syrup before. I never asked if Gram told them about it this time in the ER, but I assumed it was on her chart. Of course, once upon a time I'd assumed someone who abused alcohol and medicine like she did wouldn't be allowed to go home, but that was a long time ago when I was still naive about addiction.

Disease. My jaw got tight whenever I thought about the word. I hated that they called it that. Like that somehow made it okay to have. Like it made her a victim. I have heart disease. I have diabetes. I have colon cancer. I have depression. I have anxiety.

I have the uncontrollable desire to waste my family's money and time and affection and spend it on cough syrup and vodka while I lie to them about it.

She *did* have depression, and she had horrible anxiety, I reminded myself, the old guilt coming back. Though this time it mingled with Vinnie's outrage over the grocery-store story, and it was weird how it didn't make me feel better. I lay down on my bed and thought about that instead, trying to focus on my reaction to Vin's defense of my younger self rather than my despair over my current situation, of the havoc my mother had wrought in my life. That was what made it weird, actually. Why was I so angry with her now, but being angry with her for

161

putting me through that in middle school felt like panic?

Is it gonna break you in half to admit they fucked you over?
Vin had asked me. I didn't know, but sometimes the answer felt
like yes. Yes it would. I could be angry about it now. I could be
angry at her for being so selfish in general. But when I thought
about sitting in that car, watching her get drunk—no, I couldn't
be angry about that. I couldn't be anything about that. In fact,
the more I thought about it, the more I wanted to run.

I wanted to run to Vin.

I had my phone in my hand before I realized what I was
doing, although I almost didn't call. I hung up twice before it
could ring and put the phone on my dresser for a full minute
before I dove for it a third time. I clutched it desperately and
made myself stay on long enough to hear Vin pick up.

"Hey, honey. I'm glad you called."

"Why?"

"Because I wanted to call you, but couldn't think of a
reason."

I laughed, but even to my own ears it sounded off, and he
immediately asked, "What's wrong?"

"Nothing."

"I can tell you're lying. Did something happen?"

Yes, something had happened. I felt turned inside out and
vulnerable, and I wanted to run and hide. "Do you think it
would be okay if I came and did my studying at your place
tonight?"

He didn't even hesitate. "Sure. Want me to pick you up,
drive you over?"

"No," I said just as quickly. "I'll take the EL."

I was so out of sorts, I nearly forgot my backpack. All the
way over, I felt something like panic, although I didn't know
why. I really did need to study, but my brain was too full of
confusion, rattling with Tara and Josh and Dillon's questions,
Vinnie's easy confidence, and all of it interspersed with shutter-

shots of my mom passed out on the couch.

Normal, I realized. There was so much normal all around me, introducing my boyfriend to my friends, walking with him down the street, wondering about when I was going to have sex with him, but every time I tried to go past it there was my mom, reminding me normal was as far from me as it could get. I wasn't done with school because of my mom. I worked two jobs because of my mom. I couldn't do my homework in my room because of my mom. I didn't think I was one to blame other people for my problems, but every time I tried to move forward in my life, there she was, fucking it up for me again.

As I sat in the quiet *rickety-clickety* EL car, we slipped into the underground and I fell into the past, the foul, sharp scent of cheap beer assaulting me as my mom dropped the first can and picked up the second.

When I should have changed trains at Jackson, I grabbed my backpack and headed to the street instead, hailing a cab to take me the rest of the way to Racine. I felt jittery and unsettled and more nervous than I should have been. It was just Vinnie—Vinnie who had come apart and sobbed in my arms. Surely I could get away from a bad afternoon at his place without feeling like I was crossing a forbidden line? It did feel that way, though, all the way to his door, where my hand shook as I knocked. As it swung open, my heart swelled into my throat, not with love or eagerness but with white-hot fear, that imaginary line suddenly all too real in my mind.

Then there he was: my Vinnie. Tall, dark and strong. He looked down at me with concern, ready to fix whatever was wrong, ready to comfort me. Ready to let me spend the afternoon studying or talking or whatever I wanted. Ready to distract me or leave me alone. Ready to meet my friends and family. Ready to come pick me up or let me make my own way to his place. Whatever I needed. Whatever I asked for.

Vincent Fierro, there for me, always. However I needed him.

The fear fell away, and I stepped forward into his apartment. I dropped my backpack to the floor and slid into the warmth of his arms.

Chapter Twenty-Three

In Vince's arms, Trey remained silent, shaking. "Do you want to talk about it?" Vince asked.

Trey shook his head. Vince wasn't surprised. He guided Trey to the couch where he continued to hold him, stroking his hair and making shushing noises. He could feel Trey putting himself back together, pulling that mantle of normalcy and nonchalance back around himself. He wasn't surprised when Trey gently pushed him away.

"I'm fine," he said. "I'm sorry to barge in on you—"

"Don't be silly." He stroked Trey's hair again. "I'm here for you, whatever you need."

Trey nodded, although he kept his eyes on some distant thing only he could see. "I need to study."

"Sure," Vince said, although he wasn't fooled for a minute. Trey needed something, even if he didn't know it himself. Vince had to give him time to work it out. "Do you need me to turn off the TV?"

"No." Trey finally turned to smile weakly over at him. It was such a sad attempt at happiness, it about broke Vince's heart. "Thank you."

Trey pulled a textbook and a spiral notebook out of his backpack, and at first, he really did study. Although the TV was on, Vince had turned it down low, and Vince paid it no attention. Trey sat cross-legged on the couch next to him, reading his text, highlighting, occasionally jotting things down in his notebook. He managed to make a bit of progress, but at some point, Vince noticed he hadn't turned the page in some time. He sat perfectly still, staring down at his book, but Vince was sure his focus was a million miles away.

No. Not a million miles. His focus was somewhere over on Loomis Street.

"Was it your mom?" Vince asked at last.

Trey's head jerked, nodding as if it pained him to do so.

Vince wanted to comfort him, but he had a feeling it wouldn't be welcomed at that moment. Accepting comfort would mean admitting that something was wrong, and Trey couldn't do that. He couldn't admit that whatever was happening at home was killing him. He'd hold on to his determination that he could handle it all. *I'm fine,* he'd say, if Vince dared to ask, and so there was no point in asking. Except that Vince couldn't stand to sit there, doing nothing.

"Trey?"

He wasn't sure Trey heard him, but it didn't matter, because all at once Trey started to talk.

"You know what's weird about addiction?"

A lot of things, Vince figured, but he shook his head. "No. What?"

"The way it changes words. It makes them mean something else. Like *disease.* To the rest of the world, *disease* is something random. It's something awful. It's a bad thing that happens to good people, like breast cancer killing a mom, or leukemia taking little kids. *Disease* is some tragic, malignant thing killing innocent people."

"Like cerebral palsy."

"Right. But not with alcoholics, or addicts. Because for them, *disease* is a free pass. It's their get-out-of-jail card. No matter what they do, no matter how fucked up they get or how much they hurt people around them, they hold up their card. 'It's a disease.' And it's bullshit, because a disease is something that can't be helped. I mean, one day you notice something weird, like a lump under your arm, or something off, like your vision is blurry, and you go to the doctor, and he says, 'You're sick.' Or maybe you make one bad decision, like one time you go home with a guy and don't use a condom, and now you have a disease.

"But this? This is different. *This* is making a conscious choice, not just once, but again and again and again. And anytime somebody tries to call you to the carpet for it, you smile, and you say, 'Oh, I'm sorry, but it's not my fault. You see, I have a disease.'"

Vince reached over to Trey and touched his shoulder, but Trey didn't budge. He kept talking as if Vince wasn't there at all.

"And *hope*. It changes that word too. Because to other people, hope is something good. It's something bright and helpful and optimistic. But when you're dealing with an addict, hope is nothing but a trap."

"Trey—"

"Every once in awhile, you have a really good day. Every so often, you see a break in the clouds, and you spend an afternoon together eating pizza and talking about that vacation you took back when things were good. And you might be tempted to hope. Back when I was a teenager, I did. But I know better now, because hope is a lie. It's like fool's gold. Pretty soon you learn that all hope does is make it easier for them to crush you. Hope is like a window in a top-story apartment, and if you open it up, you'll be able to breathe for a minute, but sooner or later they'll come up from behind you and push you out. And so, you kill it. Like in that movie with Vincent D'Onofrio and J.Lo, where he knows his dad will kill the bird, and so he kills it himself instead. He holds it under the water until it drowns, but he does it to save the bird from pain. And that's what you do with hope. Because it's not just some innocent bird. It's bigger than that, and it's cruel, and if you let it grow, it will smash you to pieces. So you kill it fast, before it kills you."

Vince struggled with what to say. *You're wrong? I'm sorry?*

167

It shouldn't be like that? But Trey was still talking.

"And *promise*. That's the worst one of all. Because a promise is supposed to be real. Like a vow. Almost sacred. But with an addict, a promise is no better than hope. It's a lie."

"Trey, honey, I don't know if I understand."

"Do you have any idea how many times she's promised? How many times she's said it won't happen again, this is the last time, I won't let you down, I'll stay sober. 'I promise, Trey.' And she even means it when she says it. That's the worst thing about promises. People promise, as if they have any control over it at all, but they don't. She can promise me the moon, and she might mean it too, but when it's all said and done, a promise is nothing but words. Empty, stupid, meaningless words. It proves nothing. The only thing that would mean anything at all would be to stop talking and *act*. To stop making promises and actually *quit*. But that never happens. You know why, Vin?"

There was a lump in Vince's throat, but he forced himself to speak. "Why?"

"Because that bottle is stronger than any words. That goddamn *disease* will give her the only excuse she needs to walk down to Lucky's and grab a bottle of vodka, or worse yet, one of cough syrup—"

"Cough syrup?"

"And just like that, it's over. And if you'd been stupid enough to let hope live, or if you'd been fool enough to believe the promise, you'd be crushed. Ruined by that bottle. But I know better now. I kill the hope before it can start. I ignore the promises. That's how I survive." He looked over at Vince, his blue eyes wide and vulnerable. "That's the only way to survive."

It was the saddest thing Vince had ever heard, this reasoning that living in such a dark, horrible place was the only way Trey had to protect himself from the pain. He grabbed Trey and pulled him into his arms, and Trey came, not caring when his books fell from his lap to the floor. He huddled against

Vince, curling into him, and Vince kissed his blond head.

"We'll find another way," he said. *I promise.* He stopped himself before saying the words out loud, because Trey wouldn't believe them anyway. And that was the part Vince hated most of all.

Chapter Twenty-Four

I dozed a bit, but even in the comfort of Vince's arms, I couldn't relax. I had schoolwork to do. I had to be up early. I needed to check on Gram.

But first, I just wanted a bit of time. And if the hard bulge pushing against my hip was any indication, Vince had other things on his mind.

"You awake?" he asked as he nuzzled my neck.

"Mm-hmm." I stretched, feeling the length of his body against mine, smiling at the way he moaned when I pressed into him.

"You need to study."

"I do," I confessed. I tilted my head so I could look up at him. "But I can think of about a billion other things I'd rather do."

He made a sound, almost like a growl. "You and me both."

I smiled, kissing him, loving the flirtatious look on his face. "Oh yeah?"

"I'm making a list."

He said it as a joke, but it made my heart skip a beat, partly from nerves, but partly just wondering what exactly he had in mind. "Like what?" I asked.

"Lots of things."

"Tell me one."

"I'll do better than that. Let me show you." He took my hand and started to pull me from the couch, but I hesitated. I wanted him. God, I wanted him. But I still wasn't sure if I was ready.

He seemed to read my mind. He smiled, that goddamn cute smile of his that made my stomach do a somersault. "Trust me."

In the other corner of the room was a big, deep chair with an ottoman in front of it. He sat me down in it, and then, to my surprise, he left and came back holding a laptop.

"Let me get in behind you."

I did, scooting up to the edge of the chair so that he could wedge in against my back. I settled in between his legs, and he put the computer on the ottoman in front of us.

On the screen was a video, paused on a shot of one naked man bent over the back of a couch while another man fingered his ass.

My heart went into overdrive. My cock began to stiffen in my pants. "You want to show me porn?"

He chuckled into my neck. "One in particular, yes."

He clicked, and the two men jumped into action.

It was a porn, all right. I was nervous, but turned on too. I could feel Vince's erection on my backside. He put his arms around my waist and kissed the back of my neck.

I watched.

They were both pretty big guys, not hairy enough to be called bears, but sure as hell not twinks, either. Probably in their forties. Burly and rough. But there was an amazing tenderness between them too. Vinnie pushed himself tighter against my back. My pants were still buttoned, but he cupped my groin, squeezing gently, and I moaned while the men on the monitor continued to move. The first one had several fingers inside the other.

"What I like about this one," Vince said in my ear, "is that they really seem to love each other. I think they're actually a couple, and it shows."

Yes, it did. I didn't watch a lot of porn, but I'd certainly seen enough to know what he meant. The men kissed a lot, and when their eyes met, there was a spark there that was missing in most sex films.

On the screen, the men got up and moved to another couch. "This is the part I want you to see."

The smaller of the two laid the bigger one down on his back. He positioned himself between his lover's thighs. He kissed him first, and stroked him, but it was porn after all, and pretty soon, he began to fuck him.

Except it wasn't just fucking.

Vince was right. The two men weren't simply having sex for the camera. They loved each other. Even as the smaller man thrust into the bigger one, the bigger one's legs wrapped around his hips, and they kissed and caressed each other with a tenderness that could not be faked.

"That." Vince's voice was thick and husky in my ear. "That's what I want you to do to me."

I could almost have come at the thought. I tried to speak, but couldn't. I had to clear my throat before I could say the words. "You want me to fuck you?"

He groaned, and the hand on my groin squeezed again, making me squirm. "Yes. But more than that, I want you to make love to me."

"Now?"

He chuckled. "No." His hand began to move on my erection, stroking me through my jeans. "Someday. When you're ready." He nipped at my neck. "When we're both ready."

"Oh God," I moaned, because it was all I could do. He wanted me to fuck him? He'd said it before, but not like this. Not when he wasn't shit-faced drunk. It scared me to death, but it thrilled me too. I thought about having Vince's legs wrapped around me while I made love to him.

"But let's take it slow, okay?" he said. "Slow and easy." He kissed my neck again. "Let's enjoy each other."

Enjoy each other? Yes, that sounded good. Fucking him sounded good. His deep moans against my neck sounded good. His hand was moving faster on me. On the screen, the men were kissing, bucking together, tenderness becoming more frantic.

He wanted me to fuck him, and I wanted it too. Would it be tonight?

His right hand continued to stroke me. His other hand slid up my chest inside my shirt to caress my nipple. "Stop thinking."

"What?"

"You're thinking. Frantically. I'm showing you porn and kissing you and trying to get you off, and your mind is going a mile a minute. Stop it. All you do is think."

Did I? "I do not."

"You do. Think, think, think. And worry." He laughed, but it was a kind laugh. He reached around me to close the laptop and put it on the floor, then pulled me into his arms, shifting us both together somehow so that I was pinned beneath his weight in the chair. He bit teasingly at my lower lip. "I've never met a guy who worries as much as you."

Was that true? Did I worry? Well, sure, about some things. Like work and school and my Gram, and whether or not we could pay the rent and fix the dishwasher. And about whether I could take care of her or not. And whether I'd ever be able to do something that wasn't waiting tables. I worried, sure. But didn't everybody?

"But—" I started to say.

He was still on top of me, nuzzling my neck, and he laughed. "Stop thinking."

"You're the one who brought it up."

"Fine." He kissed me, his tongue teasing over my lip. "But now I want you to stop. Relax, Trey." He shifted to the side, gripped my ass and pulled me tight against him. His lips returned to my neck. "Just let go."

"What the hell does that mean?" I asked. I put my hands on his chest and tried to push him away, but he didn't move. "Are you saying I'm frigid or something?" He kept hold of me, smiling that teasing, smartass, lopsided smile of his.

"I'm saying you're uptight. There's a difference."

"Because I'm still a virgin?"

He shook his head. "No."

"Then what?"

"Do you remember the first night we went out? When we danced?"

God, how could I forget? "Of course."

"You told me that it was okay to be turned on. Remember?"

I wasn't sure I liked where this was going, but I said, "Yes."

"Well, you were right, Trey. It's all right to feel good together. And to be turned on. And it's all right to stop worrying, and thinking, and saying no. I'm not saying we have to have sex now, or tonight, or ever for that matter. I'm saying it's okay to feel good, whatever that means. It's all right to let go." He leaned down to brush his lips over mine. His fingers brushed my cheek, and he looked again into my eyes. "Do you believe me? Do you trust me?"

Did I? "Yes."

"Good." He began to kiss my neck. "Now relax. Stop thinking. Just let go, Trey. Let things go where they will."

It confused me. Was he talking about sex or not? "But..."

He slid his hand under me to grab my ass. His lips brushed my ear. It felt unbelievably good. "Trust me."

He went back to kissing me, pulling me against him to accentuate the way he was grinding into me. I was nervous at first, but he never strayed. At no point did he move toward the buttons on my pants, or on his own. In fact, when I reached for him, he pushed my hands away. "Relax," he whispered against my lips.

Finally, I did. Maybe we'd have sex. Maybe we wouldn't. Either way, I was with him. I loved him. So many years I'd held out, waiting for exactly this: a man I trusted, who would take care of me no matter what. I didn't need to worry. I didn't need to fend him off or keep saying no. I melted into his arms, and he moaned as I did. His motions sped up, as he continued to thrust against me. His other hand slid up my chest, under my shirt. His fingertip touched my nipple, and I gasped at the pleasure of it. He pushed my shirt up and moved down to tease it with his tongue.

He didn't have to encourage me anymore. I was grinding against his chest, panting, breathless beneath him. He began to move down my stomach, his tongue and lips moving past my ribs, and I tensed, fearing where he was heading, but he said, "I know the rules."

That made me want to laugh. We'd basically just agreed that we were going to have sex someday, but he was back to the rules. Oddly, though, this relaxed me.

Don't think, I cautioned myself, and somehow this time it worked.

He kissed my stomach, down to the waist of my pants, and although he didn't go an inch farther than my waistband, it made me wild. I couldn't believe how warm his mouth felt. I couldn't believe how his tongue on my navel could send such pleasure to my cock. I thrust against him again, and he moaned. He squeezed my ass. His lips nipped at my stomach.

It was exquisite, and I realized with a sudden horror that I was about to come.

"Stop," I tried to say, but it was like he knew. It was as if he anticipated what I was going to say.

"Let go," he said.

I did.

It was strange and new and so easy, really, to let that wave of desire crest and break over me. I'd had orgasms of course, but only alone. Never with another man. Even though we were wearing our clothes, it felt amazing. His hand gripped my ass, pulling me in tighter as I arched against him. His mouth locked on to my stomach, sucking and biting. I could feel the vibrations in my flesh as he moaned. His hand stroked my cock, stiff and sticky inside my shorts.

Inside my shorts.

"Oh my God," I moaned, covering my face with my hands.

"What's wrong?" he asked, lifting his head, looking alarmed.

"What's wrong? I just came in my pants like a stupid teenager."

He grinned. "So what?"

"So, it's embarrassing, that's what."

He gripped my wrist and pulled my hand away from my face so I'd be forced to look at him. He was amused, but I could also see the familiar heat of arousal in his eyes. He definitely wasn't laughing. "*Not* embarrassing," he said. "Hot as hell. So hot I almost came too. But not embarrassing."

It was, but he made it okay somehow. He made everything okay. I stroked his face. "You didn't come."

He winked at me. "I'm not in a hurry."

He kissed me then, slow and lazy, a winding-down kiss instead of a winding up. He nuzzled me, his lips teasing a path to my ear.

"I'll get you a key," he said, nipping at the lobe.

"You don't have to do that."

"I want to. But I also want you to know that yes, God I want you so much it hurts, but I want you to be ready. I'm not going to rush you." His hand skimmed over my now-soft cock, kneading gently against the overly sensitive flesh. "But I'll admit, I won't say no to some fooling around."

Part of me wanted to fool around more right then, to make him come apart the way he'd made me. I couldn't, though, not at that moment. I was too busy melting into his arms, feeling safe and good and cared for.

Letting go.

I ended up staying at Vinnie's for dinner that night, partly because I wanted to, partly because my pants were in the wash.

He gave me a pair of sweatpants which I had to cinch as tight as they would go, and even then they hung low on my hips, baring my ass because I was commando underneath them. Vin didn't seem to mind this at all, finding a lot of excuses to make me get up and cross the room in front of him or to follow me from about ten feet behind.

"You want to order in or go out on your way back home?" he asked.

"What, you're not going to cook for me?" I teased.

He gave me his cocky half-smile. "If that's what you want, I will."

I was tempted to tell him I was kidding, but the idea of Vinnie cooking while I studied at his kitchen table was abruptly very appealing. "Yeah. That's what I want."

"Then that's what you'll get. You want the stereotypical meal from the Italian guy whose family runs a chain of restaurants, or you want something different?"

"I want whatever you want to cook for me," I told him.

He made me seared salmon and quinoa salad with kale. I was impressed, especially when it turned out to be amazingly good.

"Rachel is always after me to eat healthier." He grimaced and put a meaningful hand on his abdomen. "It's not easy, between my family and having to eat on the fly during jobs. But I do my best."

"You're an amazing cook." I wasn't much of one myself, spoiled by Gram cooking for me since I could remember.

He grunted in response and focused on his salad, but I could tell my compliment had pleased him.

I helped him clean up, but by this time it was eight, and I began to fidget. I felt like I should be heading home, but I didn't want to go. At all, I realized. I'd studied plenty, and to be honest knew I should get to bed early for my shift at Full Moon. But it felt so good at Vin's place. It was quiet. Nobody fought or sat stoned out in front of the television. Nobody was tired.

Plus, he kept looking at me, making me remember coming in his arms. Making me want to do it again.

I glanced at the couch, wondering how I could convince him to sit there with me. I supposed I could just blurt out, *Do you want to make out before I go home?* but it felt too bold.

He cleared his throat. "Want to watch a little TV?"

Oh. Yeah. That was a good way to get us there. "Yeah," I said, my voice a little husky. Smiling that half smile, he caught my hand and led me to the sofa. We sat next to each other, so close I was practically in his lap. He stroked my thigh, then reached for the remote.

I caught his wrist and put it back on my thigh.

Our gazes met, heavy with want, burdened by caution and insecurity. I wondered if he was as nervous as I was.

"Vinnie," I whispered.

He smiled at me, his hand sliding up my thigh. It rose to my waistband—his waistband, because I still wore his sweatpants, even though the dryer had sounded an hour ago. I sucked in my stomach as his fingers stole inside.

"This okay?" he asked.

God, more than okay. I nodded.

His fingers kept skimming against me. "I want to take them off."

My cock, not exactly quiet, swelled to full attention. *"Yes."*

He didn't move, though, just kept skimming. "Do you want mine off too? Or do you want me to stay in my clothes for now?"

I couldn't decide. Part of me wanted to keep playing the virginal boy being tutored by the older, wiser man, but I knew he didn't really have any more experience at this than I did. Not with men, at any rate. "What do you want?"

He'd been watching my face, but now his gaze dipped down. My breath caught, because in that moment I could see the boy that Vin had been, could imagine what he'd been like at twelve, at fourteen, at eighteen. He laughed. "God, I don't know. Dumb, isn't it, being nervous and shy when I've been married three times? You aren't even my first guy, not all the way."

Whoa. I held still. "You fooled around with guys?" Yes, he'd mentioned that during his big confession, and I'd wondered about it, but that certainly hadn't been the time to ask. "When?"

He shrugged. "In college. Not much. Not often. Just blowjobs and hand jobs, but the blowjobs always made me feel guilty." His fingers slid to my stomach, under my shirt, and he watched their progression. "I did the hand jobs, but I never gave the blowjobs. Feel like an ass about that now, but I was too scared at the time. Thought it would make me gay."

The idea of Vinnie giving me a blowjob made my cock ache. The rest of me too, for that matter. I took hold of his hand and gently, insistently, pushed it down to the bulge in my pants. "Maybe you should test the theory."

He massaged my cock through my pants a few times, watching the action with naked lust before lifting his eyes to mine. "Trey," he asked, his voice very gruff, "would you like a blowjob?"

I nearly came right there. "Yes."

My stomach turned over. Excitement tangled with nerves as he caught the edge of my pants, shoving them down over my hips, all the way to my ankles this time. I helped him along, pushing out of them with my feet until I was naked from the waist down. I felt so exposed, so strange, rather vulnerable, but the way Vinnie looked at me, the way he shifted my body, pressing me back into the cushions, spreading my legs so he could see me, the way he caressed the sides of my groin before taking my length in his hand—Vinnie made me forget to be nervous. He just made me hot. Especially when he touched me like that, skimming his hand all the way to the tip, teasing my hole with his thumb. He stroked me a few times, not tentatively, but not rough either.

Then he bent forward and took me in his mouth.

I cried out and grabbed at the couch, because the force of the sensations his wet heat gave me made me dizzy. He didn't take me in deep. He sucked on the head gently at first, running his tongue around it, then sucking harder as he slid down and took me deeper. And deeper. And deeper.

With a jerk, he coughed and gagged. He lifted his head, his mouth trailing spit as he looked at me apologetically. "Sorry," he croaked.

He was so sexy, red-faced, mouth swollen as he hovered over my cock, that all I could do was whimper.

He gave me that sideways smile, gripped my base, and went down on me again.

For someone's first time at sucking cock, he didn't do badly at all, at least as far as I was concerned. Not that I had any kind of experience to hold it up against. His mouth on my cock felt so amazing I began to think I was an idiot for waiting so long, but every time I looked down at his dark head and caught him glancing up at me, gaze filled with eagerness both for his task and to please me, to please himself, I didn't regret waiting at all. I was glad he was my first.

Yes, I was glad Vincent Fierro had my cock in his hot mouth, and I couldn't help it—I thrust into it a few times, shallow at first, then deeper.

He responded enthusiastically. He slid a hand under my ass and pulled me in deeper, though he kept one hand on the base of my cock too, controlling how far into his throat I went. He moaned as I began to thrust faster. His hips bucked against the couch as he sucked me. He sucked hard, like my cock was the thing he'd always wanted in his mouth, and even though I'd come that afternoon, it didn't take me long before I felt my orgasm building again. I cried out a warning, but he stayed in place and swallowed me down. I collapsed against the arm of the couch, and when I opened my eyes, he was looming over me, looking pleased with himself and happy. His mouth was swollen, like someone had fucked it.

That had been me.

God. Groaning, I pulled his face down to mine and kissed him hard, tasting myself. "Take off your clothes," I whispered into his mouth.

"I will." He kissed me deep and long, stroking my sides. "Let's move to the bed."

I was wobbly legged when I tried to stand, so he led me to his room and helped me onto the bed. I lay against his pillows and watched as he stripped out of first his shirt and then his jeans. He was gorgeous and olive-skinned all over, with beautiful pectorals and strong arms and legs dark with hair. He was self-conscious of his abdomen, I knew, but I loved that too. He wasn't washboard, no, but he wasn't anything to sneeze at. I wanted to lick him up and down and show him how much I liked his body.

He reached for his briefs, and all my attention became fixed there.

His cock was only half-hard as it came into view, dark and thick and rough with hair. I wanted to touch it more than anything, to feel it hot and slick in my hand, to smell it, heady and musty and wonderful. Vinnie. Vinnie's cock.

Mine. My cock. My first.

I was a sentimental, foolish sap, but as I stared at him, watching him fill out at the sight of me, I wanted him to be my only.

When he came onto the bed, he lay beside me, close but giving me room to touch, to play, to explore. I did. I ran my hands all over him, touching his shoulders, his nipples, his belly, his thighs. I took firm hold of his ass and squeezed, feeling my cock swell at his groan.

I put my hand against his balls. He shut his eyes, trembling.

I slid my hand higher and closed my grip around his length. I began to stroke. And stroke. And stroke.

My hand stuttered, though, and he stayed my wrist. "Lube is in the drawer behind you," he told me. After kissing him, I rolled away to find it.

I did find it in the drawer. I found something else too.

I lingered a moment, taking in the dildo beside the hefty bottle of lubricant. I remembered what he'd confessed when he'd been drunk. *I want you to fuck me.* And the porn. *That's what I want you to do to me.* The memory made my blood run hotter. I turned around with the lube in my hand and met his gaze.

He knew I'd seen it. I was pretty sure he'd meant me to.

"Anything you want," he said quietly, the words heavy with meaning. Just the thought of what all that entailed made me whimper.

God, I was so turned on.

I pushed him onto his back without a word and squeezed a generous amount of lubricant into my hand. I'd thought to blow him, but I didn't want to taste the lube, and anyway, I was pretty sure we were heading into different territory now.

When my slicked-up hand closed over him, he groaned, and the sound fueled me, made me pump him hard and fast right away. I'd never given another man a hand job, but outside of the angle, it wasn't something I hadn't done a million times in my life, and especially as Vinnie seemed to like it so much, I didn't hold anything back. The only problem was that I needed ten pairs of eyes—one to watch his face as it twisted into pleasure, one to watch his pecs as his nipples tightened into hard buds of arousal, one to watch his cock slipping in and out of my hand, one to watch his hips as he thrust them with abandon into my grip.

One set of eyes to watch his balls flap, one to watch his legs parting, letting his hole come into my view.

I want you to fuck me.

I wasn't going to fuck him today. Nobody was going to fuck anyone today, but there was another milestone I wanted to cross now.

I shifted, taking his cock in my other hand, and moved my slicked-up fingers down to his balls. I massaged them, my own cock pulsing through its weariness as I heard him moan, watched him pull his knees way up, opening himself all the way for me.

I reached lower to circle his entrance, and Vinnie grunted and flexed against my touch.

My whole body aching in want, pulsing with heady power, I pushed the tip of my index finger inside.

I went dizzy again at the rough grunt-sigh he gave as I breached him, and my cock forgot how sore it was as it swelled back to full mast, so turned on by the sight of my finger sliding inside him. *Inside Vinnie.* It felt like a reversal, a flip of what I'd expected my first time to be, but I loved it all the more for that. I loved *him* for it. He wasn't some older, experienced man teaching me the ways of sex. He was Vinnie, exploring sex with me. Letting go, trying new things.

Letting me finger his asshole. I whimpered, biting my lip as I pressed deeper inside, feeling his heat all around me, burning me, spurring me on. Feeling him quake at my invasion. Feeling him let me in, encouraging me.

My finger reached its hilt. I held there a moment, savoring. Then, slowly, I started to move.

He grunted again and pushed against me. His body was so tight around my finger, tighter than I'd ever imagined. I thought of feeling that around my cock, and I moaned. I felt a tiny spurt of precome leak from my tip, ready to go where I was imagining. Someday, that would happen, but for now, I was happy to tease him with my finger, to watch the way he writhed and moaned as I did.

"More," he whispered, his voice rough. His eyes were shut, his face red, and he pulled his knees to his chest. *"More."*

I pulled my finger almost all the way out, added a bit more lube, and pushed back in. This time, I used two fingers.

He groaned in real pain this time, but he urged me on, whispering for me to fuck him, please, fuck him. I complied, pushing into him, past the sphincter, deep into his heat. I felt his prostate and tickled it with my fingertips. He swore and bucked against my hand, begging for more.

My cock throbbed now, filling me with power and need like I'd never known. I hadn't thought about fucking anyone, not until Vin, but now it was all I wanted to do. *Fuck Vin. Fuck Vin. Fuck Vin into his mattress.* I thrust hard, fueled by my desire, and he moaned in answer, taking me in. I thrust over and over again until he growled out for more, *more*, and then I added a third finger, spearing him, spreading him, fucking him with my hand.

He was bucking his hips hard against me. His cock bobbed in front of me, and I fell down on it, taking him into my mouth. The lube was bitter on my tongue for a moment, and then it was gone, washed away by saliva and precome and need. Vin groaned and thrust between my lips as I thrust into him, and I took him eagerly, went into him eagerly.

Mine. My Vincent. My Vinnie. *Mine.*

He came with a great, rough shudder, and riding my wave of cockiness, I decided to swallow him down. The first spurt of come shocked me, almost gagging me, but then Vin began to gasp and tremble, and I simply worked my throat to catch it all. When he was done, I slid onto his stomach, weak and spent and proud.

I wasn't a virgin, not anymore.

Nobody had penetrated anyone with a cock, but that wasn't what counted to me. We'd come with each other. We'd pleasured each other. We'd been naked together not just physically, but emotionally. We'd allowed ourselves to be vulnerable, and we'd come out of it locked together, gasping in shared pleasure. We'd crossed a line, and now we were on the other side, in a place I hadn't expected to be. Not like this, at any rate, with Vinnie's ass clenching and unclenching around my fingers as I traced his still slightly gaping hole, knowing I had stretched him, had been inside him. It was he who quaked and shifted beneath me, needing my kisses and touches of reassurance. He gave them back to me too, both of us lost in reassurances, in wonder.

In love.

I felt like we'd discovered a brand-new country together.

One with acres of land left to explore.

Chapter Twenty-Five

Vince felt like he lived in a dream.

More and more lately he came home from work to find Trey in his house or evidence that he'd been there, and it wasn't long before they started sleepovers. That first time, he'd taken Trey home, but now Trey stayed more often than he didn't.

Nobody had penetrated anyone with a cock yet, though Trey had developed a regular habit of fingering Vin, which was fine by him. Part of Vin wanted to leave it at this stage, because he'd been surprised to find out how many gay men never had anal intercourse, giving or receiving. For some the pain was too great, and some simply didn't care for it. On the one hand it felt like a huge weight off his shoulders.

On the other hand, he'd been looking forward to it quite a bit.

It helped that Trey hadn't taken his subtle hints that he'd prefer to bottom rather than top but had embraced the idea. He'd worried a lot about that. He knew Trey liked it when he held doors for him and played big bossy Italian boyfriend. Sometimes he thought Trey liked the age difference between them too, though he didn't think for one minute he'd been cast in the daddy role. Somehow it seemed to go along with everything else, of Trey being "the girl" in bed.

Someone had said that on one of the message boards Vin haunted, and the other guys had jumped all over the poster, telling him that was sexist and heteronormative, a word Vin hadn't even thought was real. He got where the angry people were coming from, and maybe he did have to work on his thinking. After almost forty years, though, and from an Italian Catholic family? Yeah, there was a girl and a guy in the bed, at least metaphorically.

And fuck if Vin didn't want to be the girl this time.

One night when he knew Trey wouldn't be coming over because he had a late shift, a paper and an early morning, Vince went over to Rachel's place with a pair of cigars— Warlocks, because he'd wanted to splurge—and after relieving her of a great deal of scotch, he confessed his desire to her.

She stared at him for a long time, then took a hit of the scotch right from the bottle. "Holy shit."

He glared at her before reaching for his cigar. "Nice, sis. You really know how to make a guy feel good."

"Shut up. It surprised me, all right? There's nothing wrong with it."

Her voice completely, utterly gave her away. "Bullshit. You think less of me for wanting to bottom."

"No, I don't—not less, it's just not what I'd expect. I mean, maybe if Trey were older, or bigger—"

"*Seriously?* I can't let anybody fuck me unless they outsize me?"

She winced. "Dammit, no—fucking hell, Vinnie, give me a second to catch up."

"Well, be sure to let me know when I can get out from under all the goddamned stereotypes. I mean, am I going to have to wait until I'm fifty before I get to be who I really am? Could we maybe get this settled before my dick stops working altogether?"

Rachel pursed her lips. "Will you stop it? I'm on your side."

She was, and somehow that made it worse. "Do you have any idea how hard it is to live your whole life for other people's ideals? No you don't, because you got to pack up and leave. You went off to live your dream, and you're living it. Sure, they give you hell at family functions, and I'm sure Mom has weekly guilt trips prepared just for you—"

"Try daily."

"Fine. You get a lot of flack. But once you hang up the phone, you go back to your job and your cool apartment and your frilly nightgowns, everything you ever wanted. Don't you get it? What I wanted was so off the table I wouldn't let myself even consider it. For thirty years."

She threw up her hands. "I know. Vinnie, *I'm on your goddamned side.*"

"But I told you what I wanted with Trey, and you thought less of me for it. You didn't like it. You decided I wasn't a man."

She folded her arms over her chest. "Okay, so I had a bad moment. It's just weird is all."

"Why? Because I can be gay, but as long as I'm the macho gay, not the gay-gay?"

For several seconds she glared at me, looking pent up and ready to pop. "Yes," she said at last, deflating a little. "You happy? Yes. Yes, in my mind Fierros are big and strong and manly and tough, and I don't like the idea of you not being like that, and I'm an ass." She aimed a finger at him. "But you know, you wouldn't act so hot if it was you hearing about *my* sex life. Case in point how you reacted to my nightgown, and I noticed you bringing it up now."

Okay, that was fair. Vince picked up his cigar again and took a thoughtful puff. "I think that's what I'm most afraid of."

"My nightgown?"

He flipped her off, but he half-smiled too, because that was the smartass Rachel he knew and loved. "That this is what everyone will think. I keep telling myself I don't want to be thrown out of the family. What I really fear is being thought I'm less of a man." He sighed. "I'm sorry about the nightgown."

She dragged her chair closer to his and gave him a sideways hug and kiss on the cheek. "It's okay. But for the record, they don't see me as fine. They do make me feel like I'm the Whore of Babylon for going off on my own, without a husband to keep me from fucking everything that moves, or whatever it is they think a steady man will do for me. It *is* hard, and it isn't as easy as you made it sound, not by a mile. I'll grant you the macho-man thing is probably going to be there. I could totally see Marco getting drunk some night and asking about it, making sure you're the one poking Trey and not the other way around." She leaned on Vince's shoulder. "I guess the thing I tell myself, what I try to remember, is that I know deep down they don't mean to hurt. They're trying to keep us safe. The world is big and scary, and different is bad. If we all stay in the neighborhood and do the right thing, be the right kind, everything will be fine."

"Jesus, that's so not true."

"No shit. But it's kind of like church, isn't it? The fairy tale is what makes it all okay. There's a big dad up in the sky who will take care of us so long as we color inside the lines. Take that away, and everything's just a mess."

"Marco would so kick your ass for calling church a fairy tale."

"You telling me it isn't? Believe it or don't believe it. There's no proof, and there sure as hell isn't a line of logic or visible payoff." She reached for her cigar and eased into her chair, looking up at the night sky where they'd see stars, if there were any to be seen in the brightly lit Chicago sky. "I wish there were a way to get them to see that it isn't the fairy tale that matters. It's the people who believe in it. The people they believe in it for."

Vince looked up at the sky too, soaking in his sister's words, her scotch and some damn fine Nicaraguan tobacco. "Maybe we can help them get their priorities straight."

"Maybe." Rachel reached for his hand and twined their fingers together. "Maybe."

Chapter Twenty-Six

For the first time since I could remember, I was happy about my life. All of it, up and down and sideways, even with my mom and all the hell she put us through, past and present. I felt too good to let anything bring me down. I had a boyfriend, a hot, sexy, Italian boyfriend, one of the Fierros whom I had it on good authority were hard to catch. He took me to nice restaurants and held doors for me and refused to let me pay for anything. He kissed me until I could barely breathe. He gave me blowjobs I hadn't known to dream about. He didn't pressure me for anal sex, or anything about sex, letting it all evolve as it would. Plus, he wanted *me* to fuck him. Big macho Vincent Fierro wanted me to fuck him, and pretty soon I was going to. I felt like the king of the world.

I should have known things were too good to be true, that happiness couldn't last. Not when my mom was around.

It started innocent enough, one Thursday after a particularly erotic goodbye from Vinnie that morning before we'd gone off to our respective jobs. As I arrived at the restaurant, Gram called. That was my first warning. Gram only called when there was an emergency of some sort.

"Honey, I don't want to scare you," she said, "but I thought you should know, your mom's in the hospital."

Again. "What is it now?"

I knew I should have more sympathy. I should be concerned more than annoyed, but the number of trips to the hospital we'd lived through prevented me from becoming too alarmed.

"It's kind of strange. We were having breakfast, and she kept saying the oddest things. Mixing up her words. I asked her if she was okay, but she was really slurring—"

"Had she been drinking?"

"That's the thing. She seemed sober. Just confused. Anyway, I brought her to the hospital. They think her electrolytes are low."

"That causes disorientation?"

"I guess. Anyway, they say they'll give her fluids, and she'll be fine."

"Do I need to come down?"

"No, honey. Work your shift. They say we'll probably be home by tonight."

"Okay, Gram. I'll bring dinner home so you don't have to cook."

I had a seven-hour shift that day, and I was busy the entire time. I barely had a moment to think about my mother, but when I did, it was mostly in passing. Gram had said she'd be fine. We'd been through enough of these incidents, they'd become routine.

I ordered some spaghetti and garlic bread to go. While I waited for it to be ready, I went to the employee break room to get my things from my locker. My phone was there, and it was ringing. A glance at it showed a number I didn't recognize. It also showed five missed calls.

That couldn't be good.

"Hello?"

"Trey, honey. You need to get to the hospital right away." Gram wouldn't use that tone unless it was warranted. When I asked what was going on, she said, "I don't know, but it looks bad."

I was lucky enough to catch a cab outside the restaurant, which got me to the hospital quicker than the EL would have. Gram had given me the room number, but all I could remember was that it was on the third floor. From there, I asked a woman in scrubs and eventually found my way to a room where my mom lay in a bed. If I didn't know better, I would have thought she was asleep. Gram sat in a chair at the back looking more tired than I'd seen her in a long time.

"What happened?"

"I tried to call, honey. Maybe I should have called the restaurant, but she seemed fine, and then everything happened so fast, and I tried to call, but you didn't answer."

"My phone was in my locker." I went to the bed. My mother didn't move. She had an IV in, and a Pulsox monitor on her finger.

"What happened?" I asked again.

"She started having seizures, one right after the other. Each one was worse than the one before. It was awful, Trey, the way she was thrashing around. They gave her some medicine to stop them." She shook her head. "They don't really know what's causing it, but if you watch, you'll see her feet shake every few minutes. They can't get them to stop."

"Did you tell them about the drinking? And the cough syrup?"

"I told them. One doctor said it could be related. Another said he didn't think so."

"How could it not be related?"

"I don't know, Trey. They'll be back in a few minutes, and you can ask them."

"Okay." I thought about my order back at the restaurant, likely in the trash by now. "Have you eaten?"

"There wasn't time."

I sat down. There was nothing to do but wait. Again.

I sent Gram to the cafeteria for dinner, and I called Vinnie.

"Do you need me?" he asked, then immediately swore. "Shit! Forget I even asked that. I'll be there in twenty minutes."

"Don't, Vin. There's nothing to do but sit here and watch her sleep."

"Stop. I'm coming."

"But—"

"Just because you're used to doing this alone doesn't mean it has to keep being that way. Now stop arguing and give me a room number."

I gave in, secretly glad he was coming, even though I felt selfish for wanting him there. There was nothing he could do. It seemed unfair to make him deal with my dysfunctional family.

The doctors came in, but they didn't tell me much more than Gram had already said. They didn't know why she was having seizures. They'd been so prolonged and so severe, they worried about brain damage and cardiac arrest and so had chosen to sedate her. The problem was, the medications weren't working. She wasn't conscious, but the seizures hadn't stopped.

"We have her in a medically induced coma," one doctor told me. "The amount of antiseizure medication we're giving her is off the charts. Any more could kill her. We have to weigh the risks of continued seizures against the risks of giving her a higher dose. It's hard to say which approach is safest."

Vinnie arrived half an hour later with a bag of sandwiches, several bottles of Sprite, water and a thermos of coffee. He also had a change of clothes for me, some of the things I'd taken to leaving at his house: an old pair of sweats, a T-shirt that bore faint traces of his aftershave, and a soft, worn hoodie to wear over it.

"Hospitals are always cold." He handed me a sandwich. "I figured you hadn't had time to eat between work and coming here. Brought enough for Sophia too, and some stuff for later in case you need it."

He was right. Even though I'd sent Gram to the cafeteria, my own hunger hadn't registered yet in my brain. "Thank you," I said, hoping I sounded grateful and not wooden.

Vinnie rubbed my back and kissed my hair, and for the first time in about an hour, I felt slightly human again.

He led me to the comfier love seat, which he had somehow shanghaied, and told me to eat. I wasn't hungry, but I choked down half of the sandwich simply because I knew it would make him stop worrying so much.

"I'm not going anywhere," he said. "I'm here all night."

I opened my mouth to tell him he didn't have to do that, but his fierce look shut me up. Despite what I would have anticipated, it made me feel better too. I finished my food, sipped at my Sprite and settled in against Vinnie to wait.

By midnight she took another nasty turn, so bad that for a moment her heart stopped beating. By one a.m. they had her stable again, only to have her seize so badly at three it felt like half the hospital came into her room.

By the time the sun rose, she was in Intensive Care. A respirator kept air moving in and out of her lungs. I let Vinnie lead me to the new waiting room, let him take care of everything, trying to stay distant, trying not to get wrapped up in this new nightmare, telling myself it would be over soon.

By the time Vinnie came back with breakfast, the doctors had already come to us with long faces.

"It's time to prepare for the worst," they told me.

My mother was going to die. I didn't know why. I didn't know when.

I only knew I couldn't quite believe it.

Chapter Twenty-Seven

Vince had been involved in long hospital stays before, several of them a lot longer and more involved than Mindy's, but somehow Trey's situation seemed worse right off the bat. On the third day of shuttling Sophia and Trey back and forth, it hit him what the difference was: he'd never done something like this without his family.

There'd been Grandma Marisa's fight with cancer, ending in a coma same as Mindy, except first they'd endured several surgeries and two trips back home before the endgame. Amanda's first birth had been seven kinds of hell, and they'd nearly lost both mother and baby. Not only had she been in the hospital for four months—three prior to birth, one month after—she'd needed help around the house for almost six months after before they were through. Walter'd had a heart attack just last year and needed quadruple bypass surgery. Grandpa Giorgio hadn't been taking his pills and had eaten too many desserts, and his diabetes got away from him to the point where he had to lose a toe. He'd been lucky it hadn't been his whole foot. The Fierros were no strangers to family medical emergencies. But whenever one happened, no matter what else was happening, the family stepped in and took care of them. They'd done so for all of Vince's wives, even the ones they didn't like.

Right now he needed them to pull together like that for Trey.

For a long time he sat in the hospital lobby, staring at his cellphone, arguing with himself. The truth was, he knew if he told them Sophia and Trey needed help, they'd help, because while they weren't family, they were friends and neighbors. That wasn't the issue. The issue was that once they got here, he'd have to make a choice. He'd either have to put some distance between him and Trey, start treating him like a friend instead of a lover, or he'd have to let his family see. He'd either have to not be there for his boyfriend when his boyfriend needed him most, or he'd have to take a giant leap out of the closet whether he was ready for it or not.

Vince knew what he had to do, knew what he was going to do. He'd known less than thirty seconds after he'd realized what Trey and Sophia were missing and that he could give it to them. Even so, he sat in the lobby a long, long time.

Then he picked up his phone and dialed. "Hey, Mom? Do you have some time this morning? Because there's something I really need to tell you."

Lisa Fierro strode into the coffee shop as if she were considering taking it over, at least until she saw Vince as he rose from the sofa he'd commandeered near the side window. She opened her arms and embraced him even as her jaw took on its Italian steel. "What's wrong, sweetheart? Don't tell me something isn't wrong, because I can tell."

"I know, Mom."

"Because you've been acting funny for months. You always dodge me when I try and talk to you, and you're evasive all the time about what you're doing."

"I know, Mom. I'm sorry."

Her hands tightened like a pair of vises on his arms. "If you're doing drugs—"

"Ma! I'm not doing drugs. Now will you sit? I got you an espresso, and if you let me talk for a change, I'll tell you everything."

Mollified, but only a little, Lisa let him go and settled gracefully onto an end of the sofa. She picked up the coffee he'd ordered for her and sipped carefully before nodding. "This isn't bad. Full Moon Cafe. I've never heard of this place, but it's good."

"Yes, it is." Mostly, though, it was familiar, faithful ground, and Vince had wanted as much ammunition as he could get.

"Do they roast their own beans? Because we could contract them for the restaurants—"

"Ma."

She smiled wryly and held up a hand in surrender. "I'm sorry, sweetheart. I'll let you talk."

At least for a few minutes. Vince squared his shoulders and readied himself for the speech he'd been practicing all morning. "A while back you said you thought I was seeing someone. You're right. I am." When his mother threatened to burst into maternal joy, he cut her off with a look and continued quickly in case it didn't last long. "And the someone I'm seeing is having a family crisis. Someone's in the hospital, and it's bad, very bad. I need our family's help. My family."

"Vinnie! Of course we'll help. You could have told me on the phone, you know—goodness, what she must think, not even meeting us and here we are. Why have you kept her a secret? Do I know her? You didn't have to—"

"*Listen*, please, Ma. I really need you to listen to me right now."

His mother stilled, looking confused, but she quieted too, as much as Lisa Fierro could. "I'm listening, darling. But you know it doesn't matter what's going on. We'll help her family, because as long as she's seeing you, she's our family too."

Vince's heart pounded so hard he wanted to double over at the pain, but he swallowed it and made himself press on. "Will you help her even if the someone I'm seeing isn't a she?"

His mother blinked at him. Then again. And then again,

and then she frowned. "Vincent, this isn't funny."

No shit. "Do you see me laughing?"

She frowned harder. "If this is about politics, if you're trying to make some kind of ridiculous point—"

"I'm not talking about politics." He swallowed another load of bile and fear. "I'm talking about me. And Trey Giles. That's who I'm seeing. That's whose mother is in the hospital, who needs us. It's killing me, doing it by myself. I need the family to help. But first I need the family to understand who they're helping, because I'll probably be holding him and comforting him and doing everything else boyfriends do when their partner is upset, and I don't want Trey to have to see a bunch of Fierros freaking out."

For the first time in Vince's experience, his mother seemed unable to speak. She opened and closed her mouth several times before sinking back into the sofa as if someone had let the air out of her. "You're serious. Oh my God in heaven, you're serious."

Pushing aside the hurt and uncertainty, Vince pressed on. "I am. I'm sorry it's all coming out like this. I'd wanted to be more careful and slow, but to be honest I think I'd have put it off until the second coming if I could have gotten away with it." He paused, because the next part cut even to say it out loud. "If you hate me, if you're going to abandon me, please, help me first. Please don't turn them away because of me. Help them as neighbors and friends and ignore me. But they need us so bad, Ma. They're exhausted and wrung out, and they don't have anyone but me, and I'm not enough." He blanched and fished wildly around for a tissue. "Oh God, please don't cry."

"*Don't cry.*" Lisa withdrew a tissue from her purse and wiped angrily at her tears. "*Don't cry*, you tell me. But first you tell me I'm going to abandon my son, and you remind me what my Christian duty is to my friends, as if I wouldn't remember on my own."

She sobbed once, but when Vince tried to reach out to comfort her, she slapped him away. She was still crying, but she was pissed too. Furious in a way only Fierro women could be.

"Is that what you think of me?" she went on. "That I would turn you away, turn your lover away? You think the family would turn you away?"

Vince paused. Well, yes he did. "I heard them talking at the baptism. About Hank. About how awful he was."

"He was caught with a hooker. Of course they were talking about him." She waved her hand angrily in the direction of the northern suburbs. "He gives everyone plenty to talk about. Has he ever come home with a nice boy? No. He comes home high and drunk and breaks his mother's heart. He gets diseases and yells and has boyfriends who beat him up. Then he blames us for his problems."

Vince was not buying this. "Well, in his defense, it's not like you make it easy. Find a nice girl. Find a nice boy. Have babies. Get a good job. Go to church. So many goddamn rules, we about choke on them."

The other patrons in the coffee shop were starting to watch them uneasily, and for half a second Vince felt bad. Then his mom started up again, and he forgot everyone else.

"Rules! Rules to protect you, to guide you? Maybe. The rules of the church, of God."

"The church that says my loving Trey is a sin?"

Lisa rolled her eyes. "Please. They say the same thing about birth control, and do we pay attention to that?"

"Oh, so it's a buffet now, is it? Good to know."

"You're not too old for me to paddle your backside, young man!"

"I heard them." Vince didn't shout, because getting the words out hurt, every one. "I heard them talking about Hank. I heard them say people like that aren't family. And they meant

199

that he was gay, Ma. I could tell."

His mother deflated. "That was probably Olivia. She's always been a bigoted little bitch." Lisa closed the distance between them and took Vince's hands, squeezing them tight. "I won't lie to you, Vincent. I'm surprised. Upset too, I'll admit that, because...well, it's not what I'd pick for you. And yes, the family will be tricky. Hank made sure this road is littered with trash. But what you say to me, your mother! To have you stand here and imply I won't love you because—because—"

"Because I'm gay?"

She reached up and touched his face. "You think I would turn you away for that? You think that of me?"

Vince was having to blink, a lot, to keep his own tears away. "I was afraid of it, yeah."

She slapped him, but without any heat. "Don't you ever think that again."

He gave up and let the tears roll down his cheeks. "Yes, ma'am."

Kissing him on the cheek, she drew him into her arms. Vince hugged her back, and over her shoulder he saw several of the other patrons wiping at their eyes. Trey's coworkers were openly blowing their noses and hugging each other.

He smiled. Nobody did drama quite like the Italians.

Lisa patted him and went back to business. "So you said Mindy is in the hospital? How long has she been there? Have they gone home? Do they need food? Of course they need food. What about the house, has anyone been tidying up for them? And you, have you been getting any sleep? Poor little Trey, he works so hard. You've been watching out for him, yes? He's such a young thing, so sweet, grew up so fast. You take care of him, Vincent, and we'll take care of the rest. I wonder if Flora is home?"

She kept going, pulling out her cellphone and texting people as she continued to rattle off questions and demands, and Vince simply stood there and watched her, grinning and beaming and bursting with familial pride.

Chapter Twenty-Eight

The funny thing about the ICU is that there is no time. Walking into it is like stepping out of life, out of the regular daily routine, away from a world of lattes and streetlights and reality TV and into some hushed dimension where everybody speaks in whispers, and each second is ticked off by the steady beep of heart monitors and the *whish—click—fffft* of the ventilators.

A stream of people wandered in and out of my box of consciousness: Vin, bringing me food; the nurses, smiling apologetically; people asking what we needed. A number of those people turned out to be Fierros, which surprised me, but I didn't have the brain power to think much beyond that. Vin's family was helping. That was nice of them.

At first, I was uncomfortable by their offers. *No, we don't need anything. We're fine. Thanks for asking.* I'd try to smile, then worry that was wrong, and try to frown.

"Let them help," the grief counselor told me. I hadn't asked to see him, but he'd appeared in her room anyway. "Don't be afraid to tell them what needs to be done."

After that, I strived for honesty. We needed rides for Gram to and from the hospital. Gram needed meals. Vin's family sprang right into action, and Rachel even offered to stay a couple of nights with my mom so I could go home and sleep in a real bed. When I got home, I found out they'd been doing dishes and cleaning, and the fridge and freezer overflowed with amazing, wonderful food. Whatever else I needed, they told me, just ask.

Vinnie himself was great. Solid. Present. Most of all, silent. I didn't know if it was because he didn't know what to say, or because he sensed it was what I needed. Either way, I appreciated it. I wished there was a polite way to tell the others to do the same.

They meant well. I knew that, but the repetitive awkwardness of the conversation wore on me.

"How is she?" they'd always ask.

Mostly dead, just like she looks. "They say her MRI doesn't show any new degeneration."

"What happened?"

She abused her body for forty years. "We don't really know."

"Are you holding up all right?"

"I'm fine."

The conversations made me self-conscious. Was I behaving the way a son should? Did I sound too sure when I told them I was fine? Was I too callous? Did I seem properly mournful? Maybe I should seem more grateful?

"There's no right or wrong here," Vinnie said to me when I tried to make sense of my unease.

How could that be true?

I sat on the fake leather bench in her ICU room, waiting for something to happen, but nothing did. The nurses came in regularly to check the bank of monitors. They straightened the tubing across the white sheets of the bed. Tucked the blankets tighter around her feet. The ventilator caused fluid to collect in the back of her throat, and they'd suck it out to prevent it from falling into her lungs. That was the only time she'd make any sound—a sort of low-pitched whine that spoke of primal pain. I learned to put on my headphones and crank the volume until they were done.

I quickly decided those working there were saints, but they'd lost a bit of touch with reality. "We're going to put in a suppository today. A good bowel movement will probably make her more comfortable."

Good Lord. What could anyone say to that?

Beep. Beep. Beep.

The monitors went on.

I lived each second as if it were the only second. No thoughts of the past. Anything that had happened before our admittance to this strange universe seemed foggy and dull. To say there were no thoughts of the future would be inaccurate, but it felt like walking a tightrope. They did not expect her to live. We would need to have a coffin. There would be a service. I had a brief vision of myself, in a suit I didn't own, standing in front of a faceless congregation.

No.

That was as far as it could go.

Beep. Beep. Beep.

It wasn't grief. I'm sure that's what everybody thought. It was certainly what was expected. I wondered if the grief would come. I worried that it wouldn't. I wondered if at some point it would crash down on me from above, taking me by surprise. In the next room over, a man twice my mother's age lay unmoving. Unresponsive. Three women sat with him. They had a book, and they took turns reading from it, rocking gently as they did, their lips moving, but their voices too quiet to hear. The book wasn't in English. A Koran? A Torah? I didn't know. But when they looked at me, I saw the pain in their eyes.

That was grief.

That wasn't what I felt.

Beep. Beep. Beep.

Maybe it would come. Maybe it wouldn't. Maybe it would be something else entirely. And that was where I couldn't allow myself to go. I couldn't bear to open that door, to acknowledge what might be behind. Whatever paths were there, whatever endings they may hold, whatever emotions they may create, I couldn't ponder them. I stared at the floor.

Square tiles. White. Blue chips.

Beep. Beep. Beep.

I should call someone. People from her past. The lady who'd been our neighbor. The man she'd dated briefly years ago. Somebody should know.

Beep. Beep. Beep.

My friends didn't call. Tara texted once, but I let Vinnie handle it, and whatever he said to them, they left me alone after that. I was glad. I didn't want anyone else in the way. I'd go to the hospital cafeteria with Gram, and we'd sit in silence, pushing mashed potatoes around our plates. Then back through the veil to the tiles and the curtains and the whispered prayers.

Beep. Beep. Beep.

"If you have something to say to her, you should say it now," the counselor said.

I nodded. Because he expected me to agree.

I had plenty to say to her. Vile, angry things. I doubted that was what he meant.

"This may be your last chance," he said. "You'll regret it later."

Yes, that was probably true. Later, when the grief finally found me, I'd probably remember the good times. I'd probably remember what it had been like to have a mom. I'd probably wish I'd lied and told her all was forgiven.

But I couldn't do it. I couldn't bear the thought of telling her it was fine. Of telling her I loved her. Of telling her I understood, because there was still a chance, however remote, that she would wake up. And when she did, I'd have to live with my lie. I'd have to look in her face, see her smiling and pleased that somehow this trip to the hospital had earned her exactly what she wanted—my approval. My acceptance that drinking bottles of cough syrup was fine. My bullshit confession that having her drunk through most of my life had somehow been a mistake. That her saying, "I couldn't help it," somehow made up for the years of lies and deceit and hiding and selfishness. That a few nights in a hospital bed somehow absolved her of it all.

Because it didn't.

Years of cleaning up after her. Finding the bottles. Going to meetings. Picking her up drunk from work. Apologizing to bosses and neighbors. Years of excuses and pandering and blaming every fucking problem we ever had on "the disease". It was still there, lurking just beyond my periphery. In the hush of the halls, under the sound of the prayers, behind the *whish— click—fffft* of the machine that kept her breathing, was the anger. The fury that somehow she'd made herself a victim. The ultimate martyr. The fucking Virgin Mary of the ICU. Somehow, the world expected it to be washed away in tears and grief, each measure of it ticked off by the *beep, beep, beep* of the monitors, draining away like the endless bags of saline emptying into her veins.

"How are you?" some nameless person asked.

"I'm fine."

My voice was too loud, shattering the unspoken sanctity of the place. In the room next door, I imagined the women stopping in their prayers, raising their heads toward my voice.

Grief. They'd chalk it up to that.

I bent over and put my head in my hands.

White tiles. Blue flecks.

Beep. Beep. Beep.

Vinnie stood up. He took the person out of the room. I didn't hear what he said. I didn't care what excuse he made for me.

Beep. Beep. Beep.

At home, her clothes hung in the closet. A stash of empty bottles waited for me to throw them away. I couldn't dare hope it might be the last time, because that would be wrong. That would be cruel. That would be contrary to what every fucking person who walked through the door expected me to feel. That would make me heartless and ungrateful.

Inhuman.

Beep. Beep. Beep.

"Those ladies next door brought in some food," Vinnie said to me quietly. "They said to tell you to help yourself."

"I will."

"Trey, honey, maybe you should eat. Maybe you should go outside?"

"I'm fine."

He sighed. He sat next to me and put his hand on my back, heavy and warm between my shoulder blades. I moved over, curling up against him like a kid. His shirt was soft. His body warm. He smelled so good. So much better than the horrible urine and plastic smell of the hospital. He smelled like shaving lotion, and laundry detergent, and a hint of sweat. A wonderfully comfortable smell that was home. That was *him*. I wrapped my arms around his waist.

He held me close. He didn't say anything else.

I'd never loved him more than I did in those moments of silence.

Time wore on, but contrary to everything we'd been told, nothing changed. The doctors' grim expressions began to be replaced by confusion and occasionally outright frustration. She wasn't getting better. She wasn't getting worse. They had a hundred theories, but no sooner would they present them than some test would prove them wrong.

I had a hundred questions, and they had no answers. Would she be this way another day? Another week? Another month? As long as a year? They didn't know. I hadn't gone to work in nearly two weeks. How long could I continue to live in the confines of the ICU? At what point did one walk out the door and resume their day-to-day life?

"Come on," Vin said to me. "We're leaving."

I looked up at him. "I'm okay here."

"Rachel's here now, and your grandmother. They'll stay tonight. But you need to go home."

Home.

The word meant nothing to me. He took my arm and led me like a child down the hall, into the elevator, into his car.

I sank into the passenger seat. I leaned back and closed my eyes. Visions of white tiles with their blue flecks and the pulsing red lines of the heart monitors floated behind my lids. I could still hear the beep of it in my ears. Weariness filled me, choked me, made me long to cry, if only I had the energy. The seat of Vinnie's car was curved and soft, so different from the stiff-backed chairs in the ICU. My eyes began to sting and I swallowed hard, determined not to embarrass myself.

At home, Vinnie took me into the shower. Some part of me knew this could be erotic. It might be distracting, or comforting, but the weight of my exhaustion was too much. He was gentle, and I closed my eyes and let him wash me clean. Afterward, he put me to bed. He tucked me in with a quiet devotion I'd never had from my mom. He brushed my hair back from my forehead.

"Trey, honey, tell me what you need."

I need it to end.

But I couldn't say that. Those weren't words anybody was allowed to say. I closed my eyes and shook my head.

"Sleep then," he said. "I'll be here."

Yes, he'd be there. The idea of asking him to lay with me in my narrow twin bed, to hold me, maybe to make love to me, crossed my mind, but only briefly. I was too tired. Too drained. Too empty.

He held my hand as I fell asleep. But a few seconds later, he shook me gently. "Trey, wake up."

Was he actually here? Was I still asleep? It felt like I'd barely laid down, and yet my limbs were heavy and unresponsive, as if I'd been asleep for days.

"Trey, we have to go. Come on. Hurry up and get dressed."

I sat up. I tried to make sense of the world.

The clock on my nightstand said 3:17 a.m.

I was in my own bed. Vinnie was there. "Trey?" There was a frightening note of urgency in his voice.

"What is it?" I asked.

"Rachel called."

I looked over at him. I saw the tension and confusion in his eyes. *My mother is dead,* I thought. But the thought was small, like a secret locked in a box. I couldn't let it out yet. I couldn't face how it looked in the light.

"What happened?" I asked.

"Your mother's awake."

Chapter Twenty-Nine

He had to hand me clothes, one item at a time. Shirt. Pants. Shoes without socks. Somebody who was not me put them on and followed him out the door into the cold, damp night. In his car, I leaned my forehead against the cool glass of the window.

"Awake," I said.

To taste the word. To test its weight.

To see how it felt.

It hurt.

It hurt so much, it stopped my breath. It brought the tension of the last week crashing forward, a pressure in my forehead, a terrible tightness across my back. It felt something like panic. My heart raced. My head spun.

"Trey?" Vinnie asked, his voice cautious and scared.

"I'm fine."

I thought maybe it was a lie.

Into the hospital. Down halls I knew all too well, into the elevator. I couldn't look at Vinnie. I stared at the ceiling as the elevator took us up.

Awake.

Outside my mother's door, a knot of people turned our way. Rachel, Gram, several nurses, two of the doctors. They were all smiling. Gram reached out and took my hand. I couldn't look at her, either.

"I thought about calling hours ago, but you needed the sleep," she said.

"What happened?" Vinnie asked.

I stared at the doctor as he attempted to explain the unexplainable. She had started to move and make noises. They'd decided to back off on the meds just a bit, and that had led to her moving more, trying to pull out her breathing tube.

"It's a miracle," one of them said. "She shouldn't be awake. Not under such a heavy dose, but once it became apparent that she was fighting the sedation, we decided it was best to back it off."

"She's off the ventilator," the other doctor added. "She's breathing on her own."

"What about the seizures?" I asked.

"We haven't seen any sign of recurrence."

Gram looked happy. I wondered if I was supposed to look happy too. "You should go in, Trey," she told me. "She's talking, although she doesn't make much sense."

"After being comatose so long, disorientation is somewhat normal," the first doctor assured me, "but we did an MRI, and the results are encouraging. Given how quickly she's progressing..." He shrugged, smiling.

"What are you saying?" I asked. My voice seemed too loud. Were they all staring at me, or was I imagining that? "What does this mean? Are you telling me that's the end of it? She was in a coma all this time, but now she's awake, and that's it?"

"Well, there are more tests to be run. Between the coma and the medication, there's a chance that some damage was done. We won't know for sure right away, but really, I'd say her chances are good. It's possible she'll be back home within the week. I'd say there's a very good chance that, given a bit of time, she's going to be just fine." His smile grew. "Just fine."

The first doctor beamed at me. "It really is a miracle."

A miracle.

She's going to be just fine.

I wasn't sure I could breathe. I couldn't stand to see the joy on their faces. I turned away from them all. Away from their smiles and their optimism and their wonderment. Away from the stupidity and the gullibility and their denial.

"Trey?" somebody said.

I walked.

Down the hall. Past the room where the praying women had been, now empty. Out the doors of the ICU. Around the corner. To the waiting area by the elevator.

Courtesy phones. Boxes of tissue. Plastic potted plants that did nothing to turn the thick, choking, mind-numbing atmosphere of the hospital into life. I had a sudden urge to grab them. To tear them to shreds. To rip them apart, just to feel the power of my anger, to give it a way to break free. I could throw them to the floor. Stomp on them. Crush them out of existence. Cry and scream like a petulant child while I turned them to dust.

I pushed myself into a corner of the room. I grabbed handfuls of my hair. I choked back a sob.

What would happen? I was always so calm and rational and collected. What would happen if I suddenly tore the waiting room of the hospital apart? Would they chalk it up to grief?

Would they say it was a miracle?

"Fuck!"

I banged my head against the wall and bit my lip.

I would not cry. Tears could not help me now.

"Trey?"

It was Vinnie. I didn't have to look at him to know what I'd see. Confusion. Concern.

She's going to be just fine.

"No she's not!" I yelled. "She's not going to be fine!"

A second of silence. A heartbeat of fear. I felt my iron grip on reality slipping. I couldn't possibly hang on. "Oh God," I cried. "She'll never be fine. Don't you see? She *can't* be fine.

They say that. They say that word, like it means something. Like they know what they're talking about, but they don't. She'll be awake. She'll be alive. That's what they really mean. But she *won't be fine!*"

I pulled harder on my hair. I wanted to scream. I wanted to hit something. I wanted to tear the world apart and watch it bleed.

"Honey?"

He touched my arm, and I jerked away from him. I couldn't take his tenderness. I couldn't stand the compassion I saw in his eyes.

"Don't you see? It never ends, Vin. It never. Fucking. Ends. She's awake, and now everything is validated. Everything is absolved, Vinnie, except *not to me.*"

He blinked at me, trying to understand, but I couldn't expect him to. How could anybody?

"She can't be fine. She's incapable of being fine. She'll fuck it up, like she always does. Another year. Another month. Another week, and we'll be here again. Right back here in this goddamn hospital. Right back here, coddling her and her goddamn *disease.*"

"Maybe this time—"

"No! *No.* Don't fucking say it. Don't fucking say that this time she'll change. This time it'll be different, because it won't. Do you have any idea how many times, Vinnie? How many times I've had to take her home and clean her up and hear the excuses and the apologies and the selfish fucking way she turns her addiction around on to me? Do you have any idea how many times I've told her it was okay? How many promises she's made? How many times I've tried to believe that this time, she'll keep them? That this time, it might be different?"

I choked again. I was sobbing. I didn't know when it had happened. I only knew that tears streamed down my face. My throat was ragged from the force of them. My chest ached. A nurse I did not know stood at one of the doorways, watching us. Not condemning. She had sympathy in her eyes.

Yes, I could yell. I could scream. I'd come from the ICU. She'd assume I was in pain.

She'd be right.

I choked again and put my head in my hands. *This* was grief. This horrible weight in my chest. The burning in my eyes. The rage inside my brain. This was grief, finally upon me, finally making me its victim, but not the way anybody could ever accept or understand. Not in any kind of way that made sense to rational human beings.

Vinnie put his hand on my shoulder, warm and steady.

That tiny seed of emotion I'd buried so deep inside was gone. I'd denied it and tried to squash it out of existence, and now it was dead, and I knew what it had been. I knew what I hadn't wanted to know.

It was hope.

"Do you know what it's like," I asked, "to wish for your mother to die?"

He pulled me into his arms. The rage gave way, and I wept. I cried for the kind of person I could have become that would be able to think such things, let alone say them. How could he love me? How could he stand to hold me when I'd said something so wrong and cruel and foul?

"You can see your mother tomorrow," he said quietly in my ear. "It's time I took you home."

Chapter Thirty

Trey said nothing as Vince drove them from the hospital, nothing until he pulled in front of Sophia's house, at which point Trey said, simply, "No."

Vince paused for a moment, trying to figure out what Trey was refusing, then gave up. "No, what?"

Trey's hands tightened on his pant legs. "I don't want to go inside."

Oh. *Okay.* Vin tried to get himself to think faster. "You want to drive around for awhile?"

"No. I want to go home." He shut his eyes and breathed shallowly, like his lungs wouldn't quite fill.

You can figure this out, Vin. A possible answer dawned on him, and he stilled, wanting to be moved, but he also didn't want to assume. "You...want to go back to my place?"

Eyes still closed, Trey nodded. "Please."

Heart swelling, Vince reached over and squeezed his arm. "You got it."

He kept tight hold of Trey's hand all the way to his parking garage, letting go only long enough for them to get out of the car. He took Trey's hand and led him down the walk, into the elevator, through the front door. Once they were inside, he stayed close, watching his lover, trying to anticipate what he needed. Just as Vince was about to ask if he wanted anything to drink, Trey spoke.

"I don't know what to do."

Trey stood at the window, looking out, at what Vince didn't

know. It was still dark, dawn not even tinting the eastern sky. Vince came up behind him, wanting to hold him, not sure if he should. "Is that something you have to decide right now?"

Trey made an angry sound through his nose. He stared at the street almost five minutes while Vin shifted uncertainly behind him. "I can't."

He sounded broken, and that about did Vin in. "Can't do what, baby?"

"I can't keep doing this. I can't keep watching her destroy herself. Destroy Gram. Destroy me." He gripped the windowsill so tightly Vin heard his fingers digging into the wood, and when he spoke, it was in a whisper. "I wanted her to die, Vin. Not because I hate her or I think it's what she deserves. I just want it to be over." His shoulders caved in and began to shake. "It has to be over. I can't do it anymore."

Vince put his hand on Trey's hip and kissed the back of his neck. "Then don't."

"I have to. I can't leave it all to Gram. I have to do it, but I can't, and I don't know what to do."

"I'll tell you what you're going to do." Vince put his arms around Trey and pulled him back against his chest. "You're not going to worry about it, not tonight. Tonight you're going to forget about it and let me make love to you."

Trey sank into him, but he also said, "What about tomorrow?"

"One day at a time. Worry about tomorrow when it comes. And know that when it does, I'm still going to be right here. It isn't just you and Sophia anymore, Trey. You're family now." He kissed Trey again, lingering against his temple. "My family."

Trey didn't cry, but he came apart all the same, turning into Vince's arms, shaking, breathing hard and heavy. Vince held him, swaying slightly, murmuring soft and soothing sounds, stroking Trey with strong, sure hands.

"Take me to bed," Trey whispered. "Please."

Vince did. He led Trey to the bedroom. He took his lover's face in his hands and kissed him, hard and deep. He pulled Trey's shirt over his head and held still while Trey unbuttoned Vince's own before pushing it from his shoulders. He stepped out of his pants as Trey removed his, and then he eased Trey back toward the bed.

Vince greased his hand and took their cocks together as he pressed Trey down, covering him, loving him, making a safe place. Vince kissed him and stroked him, meeting each thrust until he felt Trey let go. Vince chased after, pumping out against his lover's belly, their sweaty bodies brushing as they kissed their way back down.

Despite hardly sleeping the night before, Trey rose early the next morning. He went to both Full Moon and The Rose and arranged to start working again. He went by campus to talk to his professor about his missed assignments. He also went to see his mom. He reported that she was out of the ICU. She was talking more, and starting to make more sense, although she still had trouble finding certain words. The doctors predicted she'd be home within the week, although she'd need to do physical therapy for awhile and have several follow-up tests over the next few days.

"They have no idea," Trey said that night, as they lay in bed. "They still don't know what caused it." He laughed bitterly. "One of them had the nerve to tell me that her drinking had nothing to do with it."

"Maybe it doesn't?"

"I don't believe it for a second. She's been poisoning herself for years. Pills, alcohol, cough syrup."

"I still don't get that last one," Vince confessed.

"I know. But it's the worst one of all. It turns her into a zombie. I'd rather she downed a fifth of vodka and called it good."

They fell asleep after that. At some point in the night, Trey shook Vince awake, bearing down on Vince in the dark.

Vince blinked up at him, smiling and teasing a hand down his lover's face. He started to speak, but Trey placed a hand over his mouth, gently, but enough to stay his speech. Vince didn't say anything more after that, just waited.

Trey stroked Vince's lips reverently with his thumb. Then he bent to Vince's neck, kissing him hard as he splayed a hand against Vince's groin.

Shutting his eyes on a soft moan, Vince tilted his neck to the side and arched his hips into Trey's questing hand.

When Trey's mouth began to blaze a hot, wet path down Vince's chest, Vince clutched at the sides of his pillow. He bit his lip as Trey laved each nipple, groaned as Trey slid his tongue down the dark trail of hair leading to his groin. When Trey reached Vince's cock, Vin opened his legs wide to give him access.

Trey pushed his legs wider, higher.

A slick, warm finger pressed into Vince's hole as Trey bore down on his cock.

Vince gasped and pushed back, caught up in the riot of sensation between his cock and his ass. He stretched quickly now, opening eagerly for Trey's fingers, but something told Vince they were in for more tonight. Even so, when he heard the crinkle of foil, his belly quivered.

Trey stilled, his long thin fingers splaying against Vince's abdomen in silent question.

With a rough huff, Vince nodded and forced himself to relax.

Trey had used the dildo on him a couple of times, and he was sure Trey had been everything but thumb inside him more than once, but still, when Trey breached him, it was a different kind of pinch and push, a tightness that made him gasp and reach for Trey's arms to have him pause. Just for a moment, just long enough to become accustomed to it.

To Trey, poised on the brink of being inside him.

Squeezing Trey's arms, Vince nodded, bearing down as Trey entered him further. And further, and further, until he felt his lover's balls press against his own. Opening his eyes, he looked up to find Trey hovering over him, eyes wild with lust, smiling.

Vin pulled his head down and stole a lingering kiss. "Go on," he whispered, and took hold of Trey's shoulders.

He might have encouraged that a little too quickly, he realized as Trey's thrusts began in earnest, piercing him with pain. It faded though, replaced by nothing but fullness and tightness and pleasure, pleasure like no dildo or fingers could give him, like nothing he'd ever hoped to know. It wasn't about size or skill but about the hard, pulsing *life* moving inside him, claiming him, giving him what no other lover had ever managed to give him: space to come down. To not be the big man, not right now, at least not the kind of big man he'd been taught to be. Vince wasn't even sure he knew anymore what that definition was. This time he wanted to be the one to decide what being a man meant. He wanted to be the big man who took his lover's cock in his ass, who gave, who surrendered, who could trust and find a place of safety inside that reach.

Maybe he could write that definition for himself now because this time he was with a man. Maybe it was because the someone he was with was Trey.

Trey took care of him, thrusting hard and deep and stroking too—a little clumsily at times, not yet sure of his rhythm, still finding his feet. Vince let him take his time, happy to be the learning curve. Trey built him up to the edge and sent him over, and Vince went gladly, happily. He floated back down as Trey followed after, so fucking gorgeous as he came. Trey grinned down at him, so goddamned proud of himself he looked ready to burst. Vince smiled back at him, feeling much the same.

When Trey started to pull out, though, Vince stopped him and reached between them, guiding Trey's hand to the edges of the condom.

"Have to hold it," he said gruffly, and he winked. "That's the one thing that doesn't change no matter who the players are."

Trey flushed, just a little, and took hold of the latex as he carefully removed himself from Vince. Fighting off the weakness of his body, Vince sat up and coached him into tying it off before depositing it on the floor beside the bed. Then he slid back into Trey's waiting arms.

"That was so hot," Trey whispered, and pinched a healthy piece of Vince's ass. "Oh my God."

Vince smiled, flexing his hole gently, testing its soreness. It was decidedly well-used.

It felt good.

He nuzzled Trey's neck. "We'll have to do it again sometime."

Trey nipped at his temple, almost purring as he slid closer to Vince's body. "Definitely."

Chapter Thirty-One

It took less than two months for the Fierros to completely take over my life.

It started simply enough, with a continuation of the things they were already doing, cleaning and cooking and bringing things over, sending Gram and me out of the house, generally down to the restaurant where we were fed again or asked how we were doing, what was new in our lives, what we needed that we hadn't been given. We were shown pictures of new babies and invited to tee ball games and birthday parties, of which there seemed to be one every other day at least.

Then one day Cessy showed up at the house.

She was Vinnie's second cousin, nineteen years old and full of the usual Fierro fire. "I'm a Certified Nurse's Aid, but I want to go to school to be a registered nurse. Grandpa Frank doesn't like the idea, because he worries I can't keep up with the work, so I'm going to show him how good I am at it."

I nodded, not sure exactly why she was telling me all this— not until I realized her intent was to show up every day and take care of my mother.

She did a little work around the house, but mostly she made sure my mother got up and down the stairs, took a shower, and ate rather than drank her meals. There were no trips to Lucky's on Cessy's watch. Either Cessy volunteered to go with her, or on the rare occasions Mom managed to sneak out on her own, she found herself unable to locate any money. When she complained about being held prisoner in her home, Cessy turned into a smaller version of Vinnie's mother. No amount of whining or complaining could move her. I knew their victory was only temporary. I'd learned long ago that no amount of manipulation would keep an alcoholic from drinking, but my stark pessimism didn't seem to matter to Cessy. Whenever I brought it up, she'd shoo me down to Emilio's.

Whether my mother's sobriety lasted or not, at least I didn't have to deal with it alone.

Being at the restaurant was different now too. People had always been friendly to me there, but now they welcomed me like I was one of their own. Marco and Frank took turns nagging me into taking a job there, pointing out all the advantages. I'd make less tips, sure, but I'd save money on EL passes. The food was better too, and I'd get it free as an employee. This was the most ridiculous argument, as neither Gram nor I had paid for anything since Mom had gone into her coma. It didn't stop Marco and Frank, though. Nothing, it seemed, could stop Marco and Frank. They were determined I should work for them, and they'd use any and all guilt trips and excuses to achieve their ends.

It wasn't until Vinnie assured me I didn't have to let them bully me that I realized how much I enjoyed their bullying. I put in my notice at The Rose and donned an Emilio's apron.

By the end of the second month I'd quit Full Moon too, because I had enough shifts at the restaurant to make up for both jobs, and because between all the free food and the spare time and possibly simply Fierro magic, the money seemed to be working out fine on its own.

No one said anything about Vin and me dating, either. I tried to be circumspect at first for his sake, but this only made him that much more belligerent about holding my hand or flirting with me while I was working. Some of the family members didn't care for our being gay, I was almost certain of it, but at any signs of disapproval, Lisa came down on them, and in her absence, Frank took over. I often wondered if his support of our relationship was more to impress Gram than because he believed in gay rights, but whatever the motivation, he'd taken up the rainbow torch and showed no signs of putting it down.

That seemed to be the Fierro way: once something was decided, heaven help you if you tried to stop them. They didn't listen when Gram and I told them they were helping too much, that we couldn't accept so much sacrifice on our part. "You're family," they'd all reply, as if that ended the argument.

And it usually did.

One beautiful Saturday in October, I woke to Vinnie's curtains opening noisily, letting a bright shaft of sunlight into the bedroom.

"Time to get up, sleepyhead." Vin sat on the edge of the bed and caught the sheet before I could pull it over the top of my head. "It's almost noon."

I rubbed my eyes and sat up weakly, feeling like someone had dragged me behind the back of a city bus for several blocks. "Noon?"

"Noon." Fully dressed, Vinnie was bright-eyed and practically bouncing on his toes.

I was also pretty sure he had something up his sleeve. "What did you do?"

He winked at me. "Get dressed and showered and find out."

Coffee waited on the bathroom counter when I got out, and I drank it gratefully. When I emerged back into the bedroom and found clothes laid out for me on the bed like I was a toddler, I balked a little, but something told me to not fight it, and I got dressed in what had been prepared for me: a nice button-down shirt and a pair of slacks. When I left the bedroom, still buttoning a cuff, Vinnie handed me my brown loafers.

"Seriously, what's going on?"

Oh, that damn sideways grin. "I told you. Places to be. People to see. Are you ready, princess? Your chariot awaits."

I *thwapped* him on the arm, then let him tuck my hand into his elbow, playing prince to my damsel as he grabbed his wallet and keys and took me down the elevator to the lobby. When we got outside, though, we didn't head to his garage.

We went to the sleek black limo sitting at the curb. A handsome young man with several serious shades of Fierro pushed off the fender and grinned at us as he waved.

"Vinnie! Lookin' good, man." He nodded to Trey and winked. "You must be Trey. I'm Carlo Vigo, Vinnie's baby cousin."

"Nice to meet you," I replied, not knowing what else to say.

"Likewise." Carlo tipped his hat at Vinnie in exaggerated deference. "You ready to be driven, sir?"

"Just try not to get a ticket on the way," Vin warned.

Carlo opened the door, and I slid in, Vinnie following after. I was still flustered, but I was starting to get excited too. He got me a limo. "Are we going to Buckingham Fountain now?" Vin gave me an exasperated look, which made me laugh. Yes, we were going to the fountain, and I'd spoiled his surprise. I held up my hands. "I won't ask any more questions."

He didn't say a word, only leaned back in the seat and urged me closer to him. His free hand reached for a bottle cooling in a bucket of ice. I laughed when he pulled out a twenty-ounce Sprite.

"Only the finest for you," he told me, deadpan, opening the bottle before passing it to me. "Easy now, though. This is the hard stuff. You might not be used to it."

I punched him in the arm, but I was grinning too, almost laughing to the point I couldn't drink.

Carlo drove us through downtown and wove around Lake Shore Drive. I wondered if I'd been wrong about the fountain after all, because we were clearly just ambling in circles, taking in the scenery, like we hadn't both grown up with it our entire lives. I loved it though, because I'd never done it in a limo.

The wind whipped high at the fountain, spraying us all the way at the curb as we got out of the limousine. Today it blew from the northeast, which meant we had to walk the long way around the fountain to get out of the wet. It also meant the only benches that weren't in the spray zone were occupied.

Except as we came closer, I realized I recognized many of the faces from the last family get-together in Emilio's basement. Rachel, Lisa, Amanda, Betty, Ricky, Cora, Paul. Gram was there too, sitting next to Frank, and so were Tara and Dillon and Josh. Even the man from the BoHo theater was there with his partner, whom I only recognized because Vinnie had all but hugged them the last time we went out in Boystown.

I looked at Vinnie. He was as surprised as I was to see them there. And more than a bit pissed.

"I'll kill Rachel," he said. "I should have known she couldn't keep a secret."

The family and everyone else rose, almost in unison, and headed off into the park. As she passed I thought I heard Cora whisper to Vinnie, "Good luck."

Grimacing at her and waving them away, Vinnie motioned for me to sit on the bench. Once I was settled, he took my hand and perched beside me. We sat in silence together, the only sound the distant murmur of his family's voices and the constant crash of the fountain.

"I'm moving back to the neighborhood," he said at last.

Normally this announcement would have thrilled me, but he said it with such ominousness I wasn't sure what to say. "Where?"

"Grandpa Giorgio's old brownstone on Roosevelt. He's getting too old to live on his own, so Fina and Alberto are taking him in. Mom's been after me for awhile to take it, but last week I told her I would."

"That's great, Vinnie." I'd seen that brownstone many times on my way to school. It was gorgeous from the street, and I could only imagine what it'd be like inside. I figured I'd be seeing a lot of it too, and even more of Vinnie. I went over to his place more than my own, but if I worked the late shift at Emilio's, I was often too tired to make it all the way up to Racine. Now I'd only have to walk three blocks.

Vinnie took my hand and squeezed it. He looked into my eyes and said, "I want you to move in with me."

I almost laughed out loud, but instead I grinned like an idiot, my smile so big it was hurting my face. Before I could answer, though, he held up a hand.

"The thing is, before you say anything, you need to know the whole score." He ran a hand through his hair, and I saw sweat forming on his hairline, but the more he spoke, the calmer he seemed to get. "I love my family, but they have plenty of downsides, and we're running into one of them here. They have some ways they're set in, and they don't like to budge. They're working through the gay thing, and I'm impressed with how well, but there's one thing they don't care for no matter who's with whom. And to be honest, it's not something I've ever done except this way either."

He reached into his pocket and pulled something out, but he didn't open his hand. In fact he kept his hand closed tight, like a tiger might get out if he opened it. "It's kind of funny. Grandma Marisa's went up like emeralds at auction, but nobody ever asked for Grandpa's. Guess that's one place I have an advantage, huh?"

He let out a nervous breath, then another one. Then he looked at me, his whole heart in his eyes.

He left the bench and got down on one knee, clutching my hand with a slightly sweaty grip as he opened his hand, revealing an ancient-looking gold wedding band. "Trey Oscar Giles, will you marry me?"

Time spun, slowed and stopped.

I couldn't say anything.

Vinnie's expression changed to concern. "Trey?"

I stared down at him, scared and confused. "You want to get married?"

He looked a little scared too, but he said, voice full of confidence, "More than anything."

I withdrew, not pulling my hand away but seeking the support of the back of the bench. "Vinnie, I don't know."

He gripped my hand and held me fast. "Do you love me?"

"God, yes."

"And you know I love you."

"I do, but..." I swallowed, not wanting to hurt him, but not able to stop myself. Tears welled up in my eyes. "I don't want to be ex number four."

Vince squeezed my hand. "I love you, Trey. And yes, I want to marry you. I want to tell you that I'll love you forever and I'll always be here for you. I want to tell you that you will *not* be ex number four. The thing is, I know you, and I know that even as I'm saying this, your mind is going a million miles a minute, telling you all the ways I could let you down."

I ducked my head as a single tear slid down my cheek.

Vince reached up to wipe it away. He put his fingers under my chin and made me meet his gaze. "I want to promise you the world, but I know you hate promises. And yeah, when it comes to marriage, my track record isn't so great." He gave me his sideways smile. "But this time is different."

"How?"

He shook his head. "It just is. And not just because I've never married a man before. All I can tell you is, I'm sure this time, more sure than I've ever been about anything in my life." He leaned over and kissed the back of my hand. "It's different because this time I'll be marrying you."

It was a cheesy, terrible line. I wasn't sure what it said about me that it worked so well, making me smile despite the fact that I still felt like I could break into tears at any moment.

Hope is a lie. All hope does is make it easier for them to crush you.

To take that ring from Vince's hand, to say "Yes, I'll marry you" would mean having hope. It would mean believing a promise. It would mean opening myself up to a heartbreak that could be the end of me.

"It's too soon."

I'd forgotten I was dealing with a Fierro. He wasn't dissuaded at all. He smiled at me. "We've done everything slow, Trey. We can do this slow too. One day at a time."

"This isn't AA. This is forever."

"Yes. I want to spend forever with you."

Where had the nervous Vinnie gone? I didn't think I could do it, not even for Vin. I opened my mouth to try and tell him this, to let him down as gently as I could, but he didn't give me the chance.

"First things first," he said. "Let's just see how it feels."

He took my left hand, and he slid the ring onto my finger.

I thought it would be horrifying. I thought it would feel like too big of a risk. But as the ring came to rest on my finger, I found myself smiling big enough to split my face in half, although I seemed to be crying too.

"What do you think?" he asked.

I had to clear my throat before I could speak. "It fits."

He smiled at me again, such a sweet, gentle smile I thought I might melt. "Here's what I want you to do: wear it today. And again tomorrow. And the next day too. Wear it as long as you want to have it on. And when the day comes that you wake up, and you realize that it belongs on your hand, that it never, ever has to come off, you let me know. And on that day, I'll whisk you away and marry you before you can blink an eye."

My eyes were still full of tears, but I laughed. "Your family will never forgive us if we elope."

"Then we'll take them with us."

I examined the ring on my hand. It looked good. More importantly, it felt good. Did I really need to spend the next week, or the next month, or the next year trying to convince myself to take this chance? Or could I do it today? Yes, it was a risk, but wasn't this joy I felt right now worth it? Looking into Vinnie's gorgeous brown eyes, seeing the love he felt for me, I thought maybe it was.

He kept kneeling there, patiently holding my hand, waiting for me to give in. "Say yes!" someone bellowed from behind us, reminding me I was surrounded by Fierros.

"They weren't supposed to be here," Vinnie said, smiling. "They were supposed to wait back at Emilio's, but...well, that's my family for you."

Yes, that was his family. It was why I loved them. Even if I told Vinnie no, even if he gave me space, *they* would dog us, and when they found out I was the obstacle, they'd only dog me. In fact, in hindsight they'd been funny around me lately, commenting on how much time Vinnie and I spent together, how far away his apartment was. Even Cessy had been dropping broad hints about how much more convenient it would be if she could have my room instead of crashing on the couch.

"I want to say yes right now. I really do."

"Then do it."

Forever, I whispered inside my head, trying it out. It felt good. It made my heart swell. But still...

"I'm scared."

"You're scared?" He shook his head in mock severity. "You're not the one who'll have to deal with my mother."

That made me laugh again, thinking about his mother and how much support she'd given us.

How much they'd all given us.

"Why isn't he saying yes?" somebody asked in a very bad stage whisper, and my heart swelled near to bursting. His family was here, not just for him, but for me, and for Gram. For my mom.

No matter what happened, I wouldn't be alone. I was part of the family.

"Yes," I whispered.

It seemed to take him a moment to register that I'd said it. "Yes," I repeated, a little louder, and when the murmurs from behind me started again, I did laugh. I threw my arms around Vinnie's neck, laughing and crying at once, feeling full and rich and overflowing with family as I shouted to them all, "I said yes!"

The hecklers began to woot and holler, and soon they surrounded us, applauding and cheering and picking us up and enveloping us in hugs. Someone asked when we were getting married, but before either of us could answer, someone else asked where, which started a fiery argument about whether or not it was a crime for the church to deny them a ceremony there and whether or not it was a sin to say the church had committed a crime.

"Come on," Carlo shouted, jerking his head at the limo still waiting at the curb. "I gotta get the lovebirds back to the restaurant. Everyone's waiting, and if we don't hurry, Grandpa Giorgio will nod off for his nap."

The crowd propelled us forward, Vinnie grabbing my arm just in time. I laughed, and so did he, his hand closing tighter around mine. A whole tribe of Fierros were waiting for us at Emilio's, filling the basement, overflowing into the upstairs.

Waiting to welcome me into the family.

About the Authors

Heidi Cullinan has always loved a good love story, provided it has a happy ending. She enjoys writing across many genres but loves above all to write happy, romantic endings for LGBT characters because there just aren't enough of those stories out there. When Heidi isn't writing, she enjoys cooking, reading, knitting, listening to music, and watching television with her husband and ten-year-old daughter. Heidi also volunteers frequently for her state's LGBT rights group, One Iowa, and is proud to be from the first midwestern state to legalize same-sex marriage. Find out more about Heidi, including her social networks, at www.heidicullinan.com.

Marie Sexton lives in Colorado. She's a fan of just about anything that involves muscular young men piling on top of each other. In particular, she loves the Denver Broncos and enjoys going to the games with her husband. Her imaginary friends often tag along. Marie has one daughter, two cats and one dog, all of whom seem bent on destroying what remains of her sanity. She loves them anyway. Learn more at www.MarieSexton.net.

SAMHAIN
PUBLISHING

It's all about the story...

Romance

HORROR

Retro
ROMANCE

www.samhainpublishing.com

CPSIA information can be obtained at www.ICGtesting.com
Printed in the USA
LVOW13s2232180314

377998LV00004B/189/P